A FRIEND FOR
WHEN

A FRIEND FOR WHEN

A Novel

Gina Pham

GRAYSIDE PUBLISHING

BENICA

ISBN-13: 979-8-218-16707-3
Library of Congress Control Number: 2023905340
Printed in the United States of America

www.ginapham.com

To Vicky
Thanks for being Mom's favorite
so that I could get away with doing the least.

CHAPTER 1

My life is beautiful. My life is meaningful. My life is good until I get a peek into the lives of those who have the better things. My life seems increasingly pathetic as I scroll through other people's vacation photos and status updates about the great achievements they've accomplished so far—just this morning alone. More to come for sure; the day has just begun!

"Finished a 5K marathon!" posts a person I barely know.

"Packing for our trip to Paris!" posts the stay-at-home-mom with a full face of makeup and salon-styled hair in every photo.

"Feels good to feed the homeless before heading into work," posts a college classmate who is doing *way* better in life than everyone else in our cohort.

Can they stop the subtle bragging, already?

I guess it's my fault, really. I'm the one doing the social media scrolling. I'm the one with the voyeuristic tendencies. But to be fair, it's the Bay Area tech sector that enables this unhealthy habit. All of those tech giants, those once-just-a-start-up billionaires, use their collective brain cells to slowly kill ours. *They* are the true enablers.

Let me stop here and assure you that this will not be a rant about first world problems (anymore). I want to share a story with you. It's a story that doesn't fit into a character-limited social media post, and it's more complicated than a simple highlight reel.

You may be reading this on your way to work, sitting in your carpool, or worse, taking some form of public transportation (yuck). You are probably dreading the day ahead because, let's face it, your job drains you and consumes a bit of your soul every day. From eight to five, you are mostly dead inside. Maybe around four-thirty your heart begins to beat again, but you know it's only temporary. Sound familiar?

Hi. My name is Sue. And I, like many of you, am over corporate life and the anxiety that conference-room meetings induce. If you are not able to relate so far, keep reading anyway. At the very least, you may be slightly amused (but let's not set that as your expectation; life is full of disappointments).

On with the story.

I stroll into work every day exactly at eight. *Exactly* at eight. I do not want to give this company a single minute of unpaid time. Before I put my things down in my cubicle and before my fingers can begin to earn their carpel tunnel claims, I stop by the breakroom to get my cup of coffee. *Free* coffee. I am already here; I will use up all the free resources available.

Mary, an older woman with a wardrobe that is the envy of the office's fashion-conscious, is always in the breakroom first. I know she comes in early and makes the first pot of coffee. I aim to come in after her so that the coffee's already made, and I come in just before the other employees so I don't have to refill the pot. Don't judge me. I have a long day ahead and I cannot expend my energy on things like this. But Mary can.

Mary likes to make the coffee every morning. She likes it even more when she can watch you drink the coffee she makes. It seems to make her feel good to see someone enjoy something of her making. I'm not going to take that away from her. So, I stick around long enough to take a few sips, smile, and then I'm on my way.

She does make good coffee, I admit.

I reach my desk by eight-fifteen. You're probably wondering how easily I've wasted fifteen minutes of company time, especially for someone who's so adamant about not giving more than exactly what I'm paid to do. Well, I get paid to do exactly what John does, and I do it in half the time. Why should I get penalized for being efficient?

Moving on.

Remember that dread that I mentioned earlier—the dread about the day ahead? Right here, right now in front of my computer screen is when that dread is either validated or it gets diminished. I'm ready. I finally open my inbox. Fifty-six new emails, most of them from my boss. Validation never felt so awful. This is the start of my everyday horror story.

What could have possibly happened between five PM last night to eight-fifteen this morning? Apparently, a lot, as most of these emails are marked urgent (as if that flag makes me work any faster). Maybe it works with John, but I certainly don't need red flags in my life.

These "urgent" emails are very unnecessary. Had my boss read the responses that I timely provided to prior emails before five PM last night, he would not have the need to craft such emails after hours; thus, giving the impression that he has no family, no hobbies, no desire whatsoever to better himself outside of the workplace.

I think he's a droid. His name is Stan.

One PM rolls around and I'm using all of my inner strength to keep myself from rolling over and taking a nap at my desk. I knew I shouldn't have gotten that burrito with extra burrito for lunch. Another bad choice to add to my list of bad choices for the day. I don't dwell on it for too long though; I have a meeting with Michael.

Michael is my boss' peer, and his complete opposite. Whereas Stan likes to stay in his office and yell my name from afar, Michael is personable and remembers my last name. Have you ever been in a room with someone who takes over the entire conversation with one compelling story after another? That's Michael. He has that quality that I both admire and hate. I don't like being in the presence of someone so engaging because all that comes out of my mouth, in conversation with someone like *that*, is word vomit. Yes, I meant it exactly as you're picturing it.

"Sue, I really appreciate that business case you submitted for the new location. You provided a much-needed perspective," Michael says—I'm assuming—to me, but I'm not quite sure as I'm too busy staring at the top of his head. He has good hair. I wonder how much money he makes.

"Sue?"

Good God, he caught me staring at his head!

"Yep," I reply smoothly. *Great response, Sue. Give him a reason to second-guess why he's having this conversation with you. Say something intelligent. Like, right now.* "I just ran the numbers and built up the perspective that I submitted in the business case."

Word. Vomit.

"That's great, Sue." He shifts uncomfortably in his chair.

I clearly made him uneasy. I bet he's second-guessing his decision to trust the numbers submitted by me, someone who has the confidence of a field mouse. His face cannot hide his concern.

"Please include a breakdown of how you arrived at your figures," he says. "If they check out, we might have one of the biggest opportunities of the year."

Saved by my written intelligence. I quickly exit the conference room before my verbal incompetence makes another appearance.

Before I can make my way back to my cubicle, my boss, Stan, catches me as I walk past his open office door.

"Hey!" he shouts just as I disappear from his view.

I slowly walk backwards—begrudgingly—and stop in the doorway of his office. I dare not enter for fear I will not be able to escape within the next few minutes.

I try my best to look uncomfortable (which is not that hard to do considering my resting face screams, "I don't want to be here").

I hope he makes this quick. I do not like long conversations at work. It eats into my looking-busy-for-the-rest-of-the-afternoon plans.

"Hey, Stan. What's up?" *I'm so cool and casual.*

"I read your business case for the new store opening. I'd like a breakdown of the numbers you ran." Stan doesn't even look up from his computer screen as he makes his request. Typical.

"Sure. I was going to share that with Michael anyway. He asked for it too."

He finally looks up. "Send it to both of us."

"Yes, of course." I leave his office at Olympian speed. My (literal) exit strategy is highly efficient. You should see how quickly I can leave a room, especially if it is a room filled with people. I have a visceral fear of being held against my will—to talk.

Back to Stan and Michael.

You see, what just unfolded in the last few minutes is a classic example of the battle between the two managers. Did you see how Stan suddenly thought it was important to make eye contact with lowlies like myself? Mention "Michael" and it's like he gears up for a dance battle. Yes, I said *dance* battle. It is unequivocally unnecessary in all situations, especially when it's two grown men who feel the compulsion to "step up."

I cringe at the imagery.

I do not like being in between the two so I'm transparent about whatever the other one asks of me. Why should I cover up their ambition to outdo one another? They can have at it as long as I don't become collateral damage in their fight to climb the corporate ladder. I supposed that's hopeful thinking, however; damage is unavoidable in this environment.

I return to my desk and within fifteen minutes, I email both Michael and Stan what they asked for: the breakdown.

I used to hate it when someone would ask me for a "breakdown." What exactly do I need to break down for you? To what level of detail and to what level of stupidity do I need to convey those details?

Over the course of my cubicle career, I've learned that a "breakdown" is what management uses when they don't know exactly what they're asking for. So, you provide them with *everything*. And of course, a summary of everything just in case everything was too detailed. I already had a breakdown ready. Copy and paste.

I told you I'm efficient.

It's a little past two in the afternoon and I'm wondering what else I could do to pass the time. I suppose I could work on that other proposal that's due next week.

Wait a minute. What am I thinking? I scoff at myself. If I turn in that proposal too early, I will need to pretend to work next week. No point in pushing that out; I will pretend to work right now.

Then, I'm reminded that—by law—I'm required to take my break right about now. I should also remember to get up and stretch every fifteen minutes to avoid muscle cramps and the possibility of permanent scoliosis. The dangers of cubicle life never end.

It's coffee time!

I step outside of the office and take in a breath of fresh air. Here I am, World. I'm educated, determined, in debt, and destined for a life of middle management! Fear me. Fear me and my Excel spreadsheets. Fear me! I lift my head up high and start a beeline to my favorite coffee shop down the street.

Wham! Michael appears right in front of me. He came out of nowhere. I must not have seen him make his way over as I was in the middle of my affirmations of mediocrity. He stands in front of me with a cup of coffee in hand. I guess the laws about work breaks apply to him as well.

He is in my face. There is no way to pretend I didn't see him. I hope he doesn't turn this into a full-blown conversation. By now, I think you can guess how that will play out.

"Mr. Hans," I say a little too happily. *Way to start strong, Sue.*

"Thanks for your prompt turnaround on the figures," he says. "My team is reviewing them now. I have a good feeling about this one."

Is it my imagination or is his blonde hair literally glistening in the sun right now? There's also this little circular shaped thing just floating above his head. He is glowing. Then, my thoughts quickly return to the same place they always go when I stare at this man: I wonder how much money he makes.

"Let me know if you have any questions about the figures," I say. Then I swiftly add, "I'll see you back at the office."

I secretly give myself kudos for that response as I move out of his path. It was a clean end to an exchange that I stifled from turning into an actual conversation. *Not bad. Not bad at all, Sue.*

Michael Hans. He is not the subject of unrequited love in this story. Let's make that clear in Chapter One. He, like so many other clones in his position, is the subject of my curiosity and nothing more. How much money does this man make, and how much work does he put in to make it? I need to know in order to assess the pros and cons of actually trying harder at work. Is it worth it to go above and beyond? What kind of perks are we talking about here? I just don't know, yet.

Here's the thing: I'm only working until I win the lottery. It's a waiting game, really (besides the whole "probability" thing), and while I wait, I should do the bare minimum. In fact, I go to work *because* of the lottery. My biggest fear is that, one day, I will be out of the office when the gang decides to do a lottery pool and in that single instance of my absence, they hit the jackpot. Yes, that is more motivation to come into work than anything else. I don't call in sick. If I do, it's usually on days when the jackpot is too low to warrant an impromptu office pool.

It suddenly occurs to me that I have not taken another step since Michael left. Here I am, standing on the sidewalk, trying to motivate myself to head back into the office. This is my daily mountain to climb; it is daunting every time.

Little did I know, my life will change the next time I sit down at my little cubicle enclosure.

CHAPTER 2

H ello." An unfamiliar voice. I look up over my cubicle pony wall and this new, boyish face is smiling widely at me. His perfectly coiffed hair and earnest eyes give off first-day-on-the-job vibes.

"Hi," I respond cautiously. Meeting new people means having to make introductions, a process that makes me hesitant. I've learned that being too nice at first leaves the wrong impression, the kind that makes people think I'm interested in being friends—I'm not.

I can feel the small talk coming at me hard and fast. Unfortunately, I just got back from my fifth coffee break of the day so there's nowhere to run. Already, he's won the first battle. This kid has me cornered.

After fifteen minutes of pleasantries, I learned that New Face's name is Cory. He's fresh out of grad school and for some unbeknownst reason to me, he is "super excited" (his words) to work here. It is a knee-jerk reaction to yell, "Run, you idiot!" but

I successfully refrain. There is no point in raining on his parade; a few years in this place and he'll eventually want to run away on his own. Vigor is temporary.

Cory is now my cubicle neighbor for the next unknown number of years. Perhaps he'll go on to be manager one day or he'll quit within a matter of weeks to pursue his passion for decorating turtle shells. I don't know if reptilian art is really his thing (we didn't get into his passions in those first fifteen minutes), but if it does turn out to be that, then I will root him on. Someone here should pursue their dreams. It certainly isn't going to be me. I have the motivation of a sloth (on a good day).

I give New Face Cory his space so that he can settle in. Now that I think about it, I wish I would have just told him my intentions of giving said space instead of what I actually did: I abruptly sat down in my chair, slowly turned my head back towards my computer screen, and ended all eye contact with him, which hopefully signaled an end to our conversation. Yes, that's what I did. So smooth, I know.

We didn't talk much more for the rest of the afternoon. I'm not offended.

It was supposed to be routine for the rest of the day. Take my bathroom breaks. Pace out my email replies so that the timestamp history will show a productive day (just in case human resources ever needed proof of my presence at work). But instead, I received what most employees dread as they near their last hour of the workday: a meeting invitation for four PM. In my case, that meant in two minutes.

I do the deflated walk towards the conference room.

I enter the meeting and I recognize what is already projecting on the screen for everyone to see. It's my breakdown of the financial analysis that I submitted for the new store opening. I recommended that we proceed with another store location instead of the one management originally suggested. My work is displayed for all to see right now; so, I'm either walking into a session of praise for my astute analysis, or a session of relentless scrutiny for the next hour.

I'm prepared for neither.

Stan, my distant manager, and Michael, his threat up the corporate ladder, are both present. This cannot be good.

I enter the room and close the door behind me. Before the door could click close, Cory pops his head into the door frame. New Face is now in my face. *What is this kid doing here?*

"I should be here for this," he whispers to me as if he read my mind.

Before I can press him more on why he's invading my space, my eyes dart back to the report projected on the screen.

"Sue, how much time did you spend reviewing these numbers?" Stan asks me from across the conference room.

"A couple hours. It didn't take too long to pull rough estimates from similar past ventures," I reply.

Everyone in the room looks over at Stan, who is fixated on the screen.

Silence.

"Maybe it was more like a few hours considering the night included a bottle of rosé," I add—quite uncomfortably. As much as I don't like small talk, I also can't stand the silence.

Stan lets a slight smile appear on his usually expressionless face. This is a rare sighting, which makes me question if I really saw it. I'm almost certain I did.

"We will work on getting corporate to approve the budget and go from there. This business case is solid. Even Michael's team couldn't find any holes in it," Stan says.

I had to take a pause. *Was that an actual compliment from my boss?*

Michael quickly makes eye contact with me. "Not that we were expecting to find any," he says with a smile. *Or was that a smile? Why are these men giving off such odd vibes?*

The meeting finally ends after an unproductive forty minutes. Forty *long* minutes of people repeating what was already said before, but with different words, of course. Fun fact: if you change the cadence in your delivery while repeating what someone else already said verbatim, people will think you came up with something original. That's a workplace hack for you in case you need one. How many times can we say the same thing over and over again? Apparently, enough times to take up forty minutes.

The saving grace of this meeting is that we are now nearing five PM, and everyone is finally shuffling out of the room. I stay behind until they clear out. Well, all but one remains: Cory, who stood behind me during the entire meeting. I pause at the door to let him exit first (because chivalry can be expected of both genders). He does not submit to my nicety. Instead, he opens the door for me. If he says, "Elders first," I might punch him in the face.

It's getting late. I don't have time to do this little dance any longer. I leave, but not before locking eyes with him and giving him my best power staredown. It lasted only a second, but it felt much longer in my head. I'm sure he received the message.

It's been an eventful day on the job. I'm so damn close to calling it a day until I stumble upon a note left on my desk. I can ignore it and save it for Monday, but my curiosity will not leave it alone. I open the note and it's not at all what I expected. It reads:

> Meet me at O'Brien's for happy hour.
> - Michael

Firstly, I don't know where O'Brien's is. More importantly, why is Michael inviting me to happy hour? Our interactions have been very limited; why change that now? I reread the note a few times over. Perhaps this was mistakenly placed on my desk. Maybe it was meant for someone else. That would make more sense.

Cory suddenly pops up from behind our shared cubicle wall. I thought he had already left for the day.

"I saw Michael place it on your desk," he says, as if he read my mind (again).

"Are you going?" I ask.

"Going where?"

I reply slowly, "I don't know." It's the truth. I don't know where O'Brien's is.

He gives me a confused look. I deserve it. I end our conversation by quickly packing up my things and escaping to the nearest exit.

To go or not to go? Head to O'Brien's or go home and eat Chinese takeout on my couch? Decisions.

On my way out, I see Mary in the breakroom. I am not surprised to catch her here. It's a Friday evening and, well, she loves this place.

"Hi, Mary."

"Hi, Sue!" she says enthusiastically. Her pep is still characteristically intact since we greeted each other this morning.

I then do something that is out of character for me: I continue our conversation—willingly. I ask her what her plans are for the weekend. I do have an agenda here; I want to know if others were invited to happy hour at "O'Brien's" (wherever that is).

"No plans. None at all," Mary replies in a surprised tone. She, too, must think it is unusual of me to initiate a conversation with her. I usually don't. Her surprise is warranted.

"No plans sound like good plans. I'll see you Monday, Mary."

As I reach the exit door, the last physical obstacle to my two-day freedom, my thoughts linger on Mary for a moment. I've worked with her for the past six years, and I know very little about her. The image of her in the breakroom on a Friday evening is hard to shake.

However, my thoughts of Mary become short-lived as soon as the fresh outside air hits me. That initial brush with the warm breeze was highly welcomed. The contrast of being on the outside of those exit doors can revitalize the senses. It's that five-PM-on-a-Friday-night feeling. Life begins again.

Right here—this exact moment in time—is when I made the decision to look up O'Brien's on my phone. Something pushed me into the direction of happy hour. Fate? Curiosity? Half-priced bar food? I'm not sure which is the main driving force, but O'Brien's, here I come.

CHAPTER 3

I walk into O'Brien's. It's a little more upscale than the places I frequent for happy hour, but it's fitting for Michael. Speaking of Michael, he is nowhere to be found. I realize I'm here alone. I don't know if I'm relieved or disappointed by that fact.

I take a seat at the wooden bar. The dark walnut wood gives a touch of traditional elegance. Fancy. Well, I'm here. The only thing to do now is to take advantage of the happy hour-priced food.

After two appetizers, half a watered-down cocktail, and a post-appetizer appetizer, I'm feeling good. I'm conquering life at this very moment.

It's not unusual for me to have a drink by myself in a public place. A drink, an entire dinner, a one-person date—whatever it may be—I can comfortably do it alone. I pride myself on not being self-conscious about dining by my lonesome self. It is, in fact, empowering to be unconcerned while people stare at me as they make up stories in their head about why I might be alone. I hope their stories get really creative. I hope they involve a centaur.

My cell phone rings. It's Paul.

This is a good time to introduce Paul. He's my boyfriend of four years. Yes, boyfriend. I have one of those. I thought I would be able to describe him as boyfriend-turned-husband by now, but my timeline is out of sync with his reality. He's my boyfriend, one that is so determined to succeed in his life that he's not here on a Friday evening to enjoy this feast with me. Does that give you a little idea of what I'm working with here? I think so.

I answer the phone.

"Hello, Paul, dear boyfriend of mine." The drink is kicking in at this point. I explain to him that I'm waiting at the bar for my co-worker—or, more accurately, my superior—to show up, but that he's not here. I then tell him about my unhealthy choice of pre-dinner snacks, which I impressively consumed in less than five minutes. His response?

"That's great, babe," he says rather flatly. "Don't forget we're seeing my mom tomorrow."

Of course, I can't forget about that. He added a reminder to my calendar over a month ago. He also created a social media event for this occasion which has only the two of us on the invite list. He's thorough to say the least. The funny thing is, we've seen his mother at least four times before this. *Four* times.

"Yes. Your mother. Six PM tomorrow. Got it," I reply. We hang up after our goodbyes. In case you're wondering if we ended our conversation with the expected "I love you / I love you more" bit, we didn't. We never. We don't.

Then, like a tidal wave, it hits me. My genius brain put together the pieces as my eyes stare off into nothingness. He's going to propose tomorrow!

I say it out loud to nobody, "He's going to propose tomorrow!"

It sounded much more monumental in my head than when I verbalized it out loud. Hearing myself say it made me laugh. Laughter—that is my response to the thought of a marriage proposal. I don't know if it was an excited laugh, or more like a joke's-on-him laugh for thinking we are a perfect match. Oddly, those are the only two options. I'm leaning towards the latter.

I do not have enough time to process my forthcoming marriage proposal or think about all the theatrics that may be involved in tomorrow's event. My thoughts are abruptly cut short when Michael walks into the bar. He walks in and it's like seeing someone walk through parted clouds in slow motion.

Do I pretend that I do not see him? Do I order more things off the menu before happy hour prices end?

He spots me immediately.

"Sue, I'm so sorry I'm late," he says before taking a seat right next to me at the bar. "I'm glad you came."

Why? Why are you so glad I'm here, Michael? I didn't say it aloud, but those are my immediate thoughts.

"I left that note to talk to you privately, outside of the office." He is straight to the point, I see. He didn't even bother ordering a drink before diving right in.

I reply slowly, "Sure, sure." I sip on the rest of my watered-down cocktail. The full effect of the drink is now working its way out of my bloodstream and into my mannerisms and speech.

"I have an opening on my team for a senior analyst. I'd like for you to join," Michael states. "You'd be the perfect fit."

"Why?" I ask as if I'm offended by what he just said. Instead of saying "thank you" or being flattered like a normal human being, I chose to challenge what's coming out of his mouth. My self-deprecation reflexes are strong.

"You're smart. You deserve a promotion. This opening is a pay grade above where you're at now. You'll be the John of my team."

John. I believe I mentioned John briefly early on. I do the same work he does, but in much less time. To dig that knife a little deeper, I now know that John is paid more than I am. There's a tax for being humble and quiet in the corporate workplace. I've been paying it.

"There isn't an opening on Stan's team," Michael continues. "You've been in the same role for years now. It's time."

He finally orders a drink. Top-shelf whiskey, neat. I only know it's top-shelf because he specifically asked for it. What do I know about liquor? I don't even know what I am drinking, except that it is cost-effective.

I might be imagining it, but he seems to have moved closer to me since the start of our conversation. He's only inches from my face at this point. I can count every wrinkle around his eyes, which frankly, works in his favor.

So far, I have yet to say much at all. This conversation is heavily one-sided. *It's time to say something captivating, Sue.*

Well, captivating may be out of reach, so just go with something—*anything.*

"Maybe," I reply.

I should stop there. "Maybe" is a good enough answer when you're being poached for a job. However, I *don't* stop there. I decide to change my response immediately.

"No!" I say. Well, I didn't say it. I yelled it. Why did I yell it? I don't know. I don't know why I allowed my voice to elevate to such levels of sudden passion.

I look down at my empty drink. I collect myself and follow up with, "What I meant was, I'm happy on Stan's team." This is true. Stan may be standoffish and distant and hard to read, but he lets me be. I don't need my boss to be my friend.

Michael looks at me as though he can see the wall behind me through my eye sockets. That's the only way I can describe how intense his stare is right now.

Brief tangent coming up. Get ready.

Michael. He has so much going for him. His charisma, his looks, his ability to come up with something to say in every setting. Because of this, I have to think that there is something majorly wrong with him. There *must* be. Otherwise, life is just unfair and the rest of us might as well stop trying.

So yes, I do believe that this lovely face in front of me has a major flaw that keeps him up at night.

That lovely face is still staring at me as I complete my internal psychoanalysis of the man attached to said face. He must sense my overthinking. I can overthink myself out of anything.

"Stan is a good man," Michael continues, "but the fact of the matter is you can't grow on his team. At least, not any time soon. Will you please consider it?"

His eyes are wide and almost pleading. He needs to look away, stat! That face should not be used in any argument, or in negotiations, or at dinnertime—basically, whenever there are other humans within speaking distance. It's not a fair fight.

"I will," I reply.

"Great. That's all I ask. Do you have any big plans for the weekend?" Michael asks, switching subjects quickly.

"I'm getting engaged," I accidentally blurt out. *What? No, Sue, no! Take it back now! Why would you say that?*

My conversation filters must have all broken down. Word vomit might be followed up with actual vomit.

Michael looks as surprised as I am.

"Cheers to that. I'm happy for you, Sue. An engagement and a potential promotion back-to-back. That's quite impressive."

My brain is obviously not processing the severity of the situation as it's not signaling my mouth to say anything to undo this mess. Never ever say something is going to happen—something as big as getting engaged—before it actually happens!

"Maybe," I reply. *Good job, Brain. Would you like to expand on that?* "Maybe I will, maybe I won't." *Wow, gold medal for saying something without actually saying anything at all, Sue.*

"The engagement or the promotion?" Michael asks.

"Both."

"Fair enough. It's your prerogative, as it should be. All parties would be lucky if you chose both, of course," Michael says.

He saves me from having to use any more of my brain cells (the few that are left) in this conversation. It's over. My brain's social function is obviously defunct.

Michael finishes off his drink. The bartender comes over and he says to her, "Please leave it open until she's done." He gestures in my direction.

Smooth move, I admit. He looks over at me and smiles. He might have winked at me as he put away his wallet and got up to leave. Okay, maybe I imagined the wink, but it seems like a fitting way to end the interaction considering all the finesse I just witnessed. (That's the first time I've ever used the word "finesse" outside of a song, but it is strangely appropriate in this situation). So much...finesse. Of course, Michael would be the type to make an exit in such fashion.

Right before he is about to leave, he says, "Can you not mention this to Stan? I haven't spoken to him about approaching you for the position, yet."

I nod.

And as quickly as the clouds parted for him when he entered, they enveloped him on his way out. I'm left alone at the bar with my empty plates and thoughts (scary).

I replay that entire conversation in my head. I figuratively kick myself for what I said and what I didn't say. I rub my eyes vigorously as if that will erase the conversation with Michael from our history.

It sadly doesn't.

I signal the bartender to come over.

"Refill?" she asks as she reaches for my empty glass.

"Yes, but not the drink. The plates."

She smiles. "You got it."

"Can I also get a whiskey?" I ask. "Neat." I'm in need of something stronger as I think about tomorrow. Tomorrow, I am apparently—maybe—getting engaged. "Make it a double. Please."

CHAPTER 4

I have a raging headache this morning. It serves me right for ordering fancy liquor last night as a way to make myself feel better after that debacle with Michael at the bar. I barely register that I'm hungover before I suddenly prop myself up on my bed.

Today's Saturday. I'm getting engaged!

Well, maybe.

Last night's thought process seemed to make a lot more sense, well, last night. Today, in the light of the blindingly bright sun, I'm questioning how I came to the conclusion that Paul will propose today. After all, what kind of proposal involves his mother? *Please, don't let it involve his mother.*

My 600 square feet apartment seems oddly spacious this morning. The bathroom has never felt so far away from my bed. I manage to drag myself there and I pull myself together, barely passing the this-is-good-enough bar.

It is one of those days when I need my outer appearance to make up for how terrible I feel on the inside. Unfortunately, that doesn't seem to be happening today. Since my face screams, "in need of some help," I will rely on some sunglasses to cover up this look of death.

This is good enough.

Coffee. Must get some.

I must have teleported to the coffee shop because I don't remember how I got here so quickly. The person in front of me is putting in a tall order. A *very* tall order. I normally have patience for this, but today, nobody should get in between me and my coffee.

If this person in front of me could hear the thoughts that are running through my head, he'd order with much more speed. How many ways can you kick someone? Twenty-six (and counting).

He must have heard my inner thoughts because he turns around swiftly and meets my sunglasses. Cory, the new kid at work, has invaded my space—once again. He gives me a wide smile.

This scenario is one of life's unfunny jokes, like an unsolicited dad joke. No thank you. Not today.

"Why?" I blurt. I said it more as a statement than a question. It's a Saturday. This is *my* coffee shop. I should not be reminded of work here and now. There are only a few safe, work-free zones in my life: my apartment, my doctor's office, and this coffee shop.

"Nice to see you too," he replies.

I slowly push him aside, erasing his existence from my line of sight, and I proceed to order my coffee. When I finish my very easy, very short order, he is right there behind me, ready to greet me again.

"Friendly advice: sunglasses indoors are not a good look," he says as he sips the drink that took him ten painfully long minutes to order earlier.

I chuckle. I cannot agree more with that statement, but today's hangover called for desperate measures. I pull my sunglasses down the bridge of my nose.

He immediately exclaims, "Good, God! You look like…you need those sunglasses on."

I let out a laugh. It was more of a snort. That's what I like to call a laugh that unintentionally escaped. At least the kid is honest. I give him an I-told-you-so shrug.

Sunglasses back on. I put up a peace sign to bid him adieu (because I might as well complete this look by saying goodbye in such fashion). Whereas most people would leave it at that, Cory decides it is best to continue walking beside me toward the exit, out the building, and into the world outside.

He smiles and says, "I obviously cannot leave you in this state." He looks me up and down. "This is clearly a cry for help."

I stare at him, speechless, really. I don't tell him to leave me alone because I don't actually mind his presence right now, even in my present state of all kinds of nauseousness. No one is more surprised about the state of my own feelings than I am. I don't know what it is, but he is neither pompous nor annoying. Good qualities in my book, I suppose.

"Don't you have somewhere to be?" I ask. "Video game tournament? Boy scout meeting?"

"I got those out of the way before I came here," he answers.

I am secretly amused by his response. I walk. He continues to follow.

"And you?" he asks.

"Later today, I'm going to be proposed to," I reply without thinking. I admit my response came across a little too stoic. Crying, smiling, or anything other than the blank face I gave would have been more fitting to support the words that just left my mouth so casually. Perhaps it was because I already blurted this out once, the second time seems less important.

Cory stops walking and turns his body to face me directly. We stand toe to toe. "You look very excited about this proposal," he says. The sarcasm does not go unnoticed.

"I am. I will be. Once this morning 'haze' blows over, I will be," I reply. Again, emotionless.

"I look more excited when I'm getting teeth pulled," Cory replies.

"Well, it must be exciting when your baby teeth finally wiggle."

He seems to like what I just said. He smiles too widely at my response.

I take notice of his perfect teeth. It occurs to me that this is the first time I've really looked at Cory. Sure, I've seen him before; we just met yesterday. But right now, out from under the office fluorescent lights, I can *see him*, see him. He looks like he can be part of a K-POP boy band—an older, more seasoned K-POP boy band. Trust me, there's a difference. That is my only takeaway after staring at him for a full minute. (For those who are less attuned to the pop culture scene, K-POP refers to Korean pop music that originates from South Korea).

"Cory," I say as I move in a little closer to his face, "listen to me carefully. On my spectrum of emotions, this is the most excited I'll ever be. This, here, is the look of a woman who cannot contain her excitement. You, on the other hand, may jump up and down, or giggle—"

"I don't giggle. I don't do that," he interjects as manly as he can muster.

"Or cry," I continue. "That's okay. That's you. But for someone who is as cool, calm, and old as I am, I do not express myself in that way anymore."

"Fair enough," Cory says. "Can I just state an observation?"

I give him my best indifferent face, but I suppose I am curious about what he has to say.

"I'll take that as a 'yes'," he says. "Based on how you talk about this 'proposal'"—yes, he used air quotes—"I imagine it has something to do with why you are clearly hungover today. Hangovers are usually due to celebrating or commiserating a little too hard. For you, I'd say it's the latter. So, Sue, why did you throw yourself a pity party before your big day?"

I think this is what kids today describe as a "mic drop" moment, when a point is so well made it leaves no room for rebuttal. I cannot stand that this astute observation is coming from the babyface standing before me.

I open my mouth to speak but cannot find the words to complete a proper thought.

I respond with, "Ha." That was the best I could come up with at that moment. I down my cup of coffee in seconds. "Well, this has been a great session," I say. "Send me the bill."

"This one's free. You can't afford me anyway."

I walk away from Cory. I'm hours away from my "proposal" (yes, I'm using quotes too), yet I'm fixated on this unexpected run-in with Cory. I'm also thinking it's time to find a new coffee shop. This one is now tainted.

When a person enters your life, you don't know how long they'll stay or what they will do to your life during that stay. I met Cory at work on a Friday afternoon. Today is Saturday.

So, it begins.

CHAPTER 5

Monday morning arrived sooner than I was ready for. The Sunday blues started on Saturday night. I am convinced that by the end of my corporate career, the Sunday blues would creep up as early as Friday, immediately after five PM.

The weekend came and went, and there is no ring on my finger. My boyfriend, Paul, did indeed plan an elaborate event—it just wasn't for me. His mother, however, had an amazing 60th birthday party. When the lights dimmed and the music started, I admit my heart began pounding as I thought that this was it—he's going to propose! My face lost most of its color when, instead, Paul and his three brothers came out and performed a full-blown dance routine for their beloved mother. It was very well choreographed. Silly me for thinking he spent all that time planning a marriage proposal instead.

Don't misunderstand. My proposal *did* happen; it just happened with much less fanfare.

* * *

After the birthday party was over, and his mother retired for the night after drinking a surprisingly abundant amount of alcohol, Paul drove me home. Right before we got to my apartment building, he pulled over to the side of the road, turned off the music, and pulled out a ring. He presented the most beautiful diamond ring, and then followed it up with the most matter-of-fact proposal in the history of all marriage proposals. Are you ready for it?

Paul goes on to say—not ask—say, "It's about time. Let's do this."

Queue the soundtrack to a depressing film, the kind that is long and drawn-out with an inconclusive ending (some call it artsy; I call it someone's sick joke). I'm left confused and unsatisfied. These were not the feelings I anticipated having after being proposed to.

Since Paul didn't exactly ask me to marry him, I didn't say yes. In fact, I didn't say anything at all. I took a deep breath, looked at him with my most inexpressive expression—like the kind one would have when they are staring at running water—and I got out of the car to walk the rest of the way home. To add insult to injury, I could feel Paul's eyes on me as I walked away, but he never came after me. Not even a holler from where he sat.

We both knew that this was the end. It was the end for some time; this failure of a proposal just solidified it.

Quick public service announcement: if the word "love" does not pop up anywhere in your marriage proposal speech, question everything about that relationship.

* * *

So, hello, Monday. Here we are again. I hope you treat me kindly.

I arrive at my desk and there's a card placed on my keyboard. It's little too early for surprises; it's only been two hours into my workday (and yes, I came in late today). I'm almost hesitant to open it, but I'm secretly hoping it's some petty cash for absolutely no reason at all. One could dream, right?

Cory pops up from behind our shared cubicle wall. "I saw Michael put it there," he says.

I'm beginning to think that this is sort of Cory's "thing"—to pop up at unexpected places and times. I guess we all need a hobby.

I open the card and a four-letter word that starts with "f" immediately escapes my lips. It is a card to congratulate me on my engagement, the one that didn't happen as you now know. It wouldn't have been so bad had Michael not gotten most of the office to sign the card. News spread fast around here. That four-letter "f" word resurfaces again.

"I didn't want to sign it," Cory says. "It seemed…presumptuous."

I didn't realize he was standing there watching me. He must have seen the dread on my face as I was silently reading the card.

I catch him looking at my ring finger.

"Are you okay?" he asks. The sincerity of that question is evident in his tone.

"I was fine until I got this card," I reply a little sadder than I wanted to convey. I place my head down on my desk. I just need a moment.

It took all of my willpower to sit up in my chair again. I abruptly turn to Cory. "You knew I was going to say 'No.'"

"*You* knew you were going to say 'No,'" he replies. *Smart ass.*

He isn't wrong though. I flash back to our quick exchange at the coffee shop. Our conversation played repeatedly in my mind since that day. I knew Cory was right. I wasn't excited about the marriage proposal because, well, I wasn't excited about the marriage. I couldn't even fake the excitement. I supposed I was just reluctant to take any advice from Cory, someone who looks like he belongs on a t-ball team. But, in the end, he was right.

Of course, I didn't tell him that. There is a more pressing matter at hand. It's time to do damage control. I head straight to Michael's office.

I find Michael at his desk. He had just reached for the phone, but he promptly puts it down when he sees me. I walk in with the card in hand. Before I can say anything, he walks around his desk and casually leans against the front of it as he smiles at me. His smile runs from ear to ear. This kind of attentiveness is distracting. I almost forgot the purpose of my visit.

"Sue, I was thinking about you all weekend," Michael says. Now, without context, what he just said could be taken as flirtation. But he did start out his weekend with me—and all of my awkwardness—at the bar. I know that I can make a lasting impression (usually not the kind I want to make, but it will burn into your brain). He has an agenda, I tell myself. This is not flirtation.

"So, let's see it," Michael continues.

I hold up my left hand to show him my ringless finger. "I didn't say 'yes.'"

For the first time since I've worked with him, he didn't have an immediate response. No witty comeback. No insightful quip. Did I break him? The smile is gone from his face. He simply stands there with a look of pity, which sometimes can be confused with longingness, but again, context matters here. I know better.

"I figured you made him the luckiest man," he finally says. And there it is! True Michael style returns.

"I think I did," I reply. "He dodged a bullet." I may not always be good with my words, but self-deprecation comes easily for me.

The smile slowly reappears on his clean-shaven face. I hand him the card.

"More like, he let a unicorn escape." There he goes again. This man has no off button. "I will make sure to clear the air," he says, holding up the card. "I just wish I wasn't so diligent about getting people to sign this."

"Yes, me too." I wholeheartedly agree. Diligence can be wasted effort at times.

"About the other thing we talked about. Did you think about accepting—"

Stan suddenly enters the room.

He must have sensed that I was consorting with the enemy. His Spidey sense found me in Michael's office, and he needed to reel me back onto his side.

"We have a problem," Stan says as he eyes Michael and then directs his attention to me. *Well, good morning to you too, Stan.*

I love these issues that pop up so early in the day.

I should have stayed home. Maybe it's not too late to fake an illness.

I promptly leave Michael's office and follow Stan into his.

Did I mention already that I dread Mondays? Well, I'm about to also dread Tuesdays, Wednesdays—the entire week, actually. It's about to be one of those work weeks, the kind that makes me question all of my life choices that eventually led me here.

CHAPTER 6

S tan briefs me on the problem as soon as we enter his office. Turns out, John, the other analyst on my team, opened an email attachment that contained a virus. Apparently, our IT department wasn't prepared for an infiltration of all files on our servers. In other words, all work is lost. All. Everything.

They traced the virus back to a single download that came from John's computer. The office is currently taking bets on which enticing email subject line convinced John to click on the link. My guess is that it had something to do with a little magical pill that would solve all of his problems. Or it was a video of a puppy doing the cute things that puppies do. I mean, who wouldn't click on that?

Because John was so click-happy, the financial report that I so diligently submitted last week is gone. Poof. Gone. Just like that. I'm really hating John right now. And those darn puppy videos.

Stan stayed late with me almost every night this week to recreate my report from scratch. We have a deadline to meet, and he has a lot riding on this proposal. I'm sure it involves some kind of promotion for him if the new store opening becomes a success. Whatever the reason, he's been by my side to help in any way that he could.

It's now Thursday night. Stan is working on one end of the conference room table while I'm on the other. There are several semi-empty Chinese food takeout boxes in between us. I can't believe it's already past six PM. This goes against my strong work ethic of never putting in extra hours. The free dinner does not make up for it at all, no matter how incredibly delightful the potstickers may be.

We both have been staring at our laptop screens for the past few hours, hardly taking breaks and speaking only when we need information from the other. We finally completed our report and passed it onto Michael's team for review about an hour ago. Now, we're just waiting around until the review is complete and then we can both go home and forget all about this dreadful week.

I see an extra eggroll on the table. Well, it's not really an extra one. It's Stan's. He didn't eat it (yet). It's calling me. Instead of asking Stan if he wants the last one, I go for it. I slowly reach out my arm to grab it as I stare at Stan working away on his laptop. He's probably drafting up urgent emails—to me—at this very moment.

From across the conference room table, I could see the exhaustion on his face. If there is one emotion Stan is good at emoting, it's that: exhaustion. As I'm sitting here studying him, I start to wonder why he's not married yet, or why he doesn't have a girlfriend (or boyfriend). He's not a repulsive-looking man.

Time out. I realize that describing someone in that manner is not exactly a compliment. If someone ever described me as "not repulsive-looking," I would cry while eating an excessive amount of popcorn chicken under my blanket, in the dark, alone in my apartment for a few consecutive weekends. I am an adult, and that is how I deal with criticism.

Truthfully, Stan deserves more credit than that. He's better than "not repulsive." He wears his face bare on most days, but I imagine he would have a full beard based on the presence of his five o'clock shadow right now. He doesn't show up to the office in a suit and tie like Michael does every day; Stan is a little more understated with his office attire. He's the type to roll up the sleeves of his dress shirt, perhaps to appear less corporate on purpose. Every day, he wears an old baseball cap, a faded Oakland A's cap. He usually takes it off just before he enters the building and fixes his dark hair by simply running his hands through it as you might picture a little boy would. When you work with someone for a long time, you develop a mental catalogue of little details about them.

I obviously must not have enough to do at work.

I take a bite of the eggroll. The crunch must have snapped Stan out of his work mode. He looks up from over his laptop screen and says, "Congratulations, Sue. I heard about the engagement."

Ladies and gentlemen, hell must have frozen over. Stanley Edwards, the man who has not once engaged in small talk with me in the six years that I've worked for him, has finally spoken to me about something non-work related. Let it be known that at 6:41 PM on this day, I started to believe in miracles.

I am so taken aback by his remark that half of the eggroll fell out of my mouth as I try to speak (yours truly strikes again). That, right there, is probably the reason why Stan and I never had a real conversation. My awkwardness can repel some people or invade their personal space like some kind of contagion.

I'm a stranger to grace.

Stan looks down immediately as if to pretend he didn't witness my blunder. However, he is unsuccessful at hiding that slight smile on his face.

Ladies and gentlemen, is he being considerate, as well? I thought that our biggest problem at work is the virus that wiped out all of our data, but I think this network virus got to my boss too. He must be broken. He is infected.

I finally reply, "The engagement didn't happen. What I mean is, it *did* happen, but I said 'no.'"

"Why?"

I can't believe he's asking follow-up questions. I am not prepared for this. *Okay, Stanley Edwards. Let's do this. Let's get deep. I'll entertain this version of you while it lasts.*

However, I didn't exactly know how to answer the 'why' in his question.

"He told me it was time to get married," I say.

"And you didn't agree?" Stan asks.

"It was time, yes. But that can't be the only reason to get married." I feel I may be oversharing, but I continue. "I wanted to feel *something*."

"Like love? Passion?"

I chuckle, almost snort. "What would you know about passion?" I can't help myself; it is an honest reaction to hearing Stan utter those words, which didn't sound natural coming from someone with a limited range of emotions.

He looks semi-hurt at my response, yet I don't stop there. I continue, "You just seem so—"

"Robotic?" he says, finishing my thought for me. At least he's self-aware.

"I was going to say 'heartless,' but yes. 'Robotic' is fitting," I say. "Are you even capable of love? Have you ever been in love, Stan?"

At this point, I feel I may have crossed the line. Maybe it's time to dial it back a bit. He is still my boss, after all.

His face changes drastically from seconds before. Instead of a verbal response, Stan softens his stare and holds his gaze on me. This is the first time—ever—that I see some gentleness in his brown eyes. It is also the first time I realize his eyes are light brown with specks of gold (that should tell you how often we make eye contact). I will add this newly discovered detail about his eyes into my mental catalogue. Light brown and gold.

He lets out a deep breath and relaxes his shoulders. He's looking directly at me but he's thinking and seeing a million different things in his head.

The look on his face is one that I cannot easily break away from.

Flush. That's what I feel. I can *feel* the color red upon my cheeks. I can't move, much less breathe. I deliberately adjust my sitting posture as a reason to look away. When I look up again, he quickly shifts his eyes elsewhere.

What just happened here? What is this moment that passed between us? Was it even a moment? I am just as confused as you are, dear readers. It's ironic that this heartless robot of a man is able to cause *my* heart to palpitate so much so that I feel myself trembling.

Did I already mention that I cannot breathe? It's too hot—no, it's too cold in here. My body must be confused about how to react in this situation. It's trying to triage something that is unfamiliar. Brain is losing function; body is shutting down.

I might be dying.

"Sue…" Stan gently says. I see the apprehension on his face. He looks down and swallows the words he wanted to say.

Suddenly, the door of the conference room swings wide open, and Cory walks in.

"What are you two still doing here?" Cory says as he puts a fistful of popcorn into his mouth.

I have never been more thankful to see Cory's stupidly happy face than I am right now. This kid has grown on me tenfold just in this instance alone.

"We're waiting on Michael's team to finish up the review," Stan says in his most professional voice. "Waiting on some feedback." And just like that, Stan switched from almost human back to droid boss mode.

"Michael's team isn't here anymore," Cory says as he shoves another handful of popcorn into his mouth. "I heard they already submitted version two of the report to corporate." Popcorn everywhere. Cory doesn't seem to notice.

Stan and I immediately give each other a look. It is certainly not the same look that passed between us just moments earlier. It is now a look of exhaustion mixed with a bit of annoyance. We are both ready to go home. I am ready to flee the scene as if I'd done something wrong.

I quickly pack up my things and head for the door. I shuffle Cory along my way out. More popcorn everywhere. He bends down and tries to pick them up one by one. *Now* he notices the mess he made. Poor timing. I need to make my swift escape. I turn the shuffling into pushing and I successfully escort Cory out the door without much opposition.

I didn't realize that I had a death grip on Cory's arm as we speed walked down the hallway. I want to hang onto Cory a little longer until I can completely escape Stan's presence for the night. I need him for support as I am obviously unstable (in more ways than one).

We're almost near the breakroom when he finally whispers to me, "You are shaking. What happened back there?"

"Exhaustion. I'm dying," I reply flatly as I scan the hallway. My eyes dart back and forth in hopes of no sighting of Stan behind us. All clear for now.

"You say things in monotone and with such a blank face, I don't know when you're serious, Sue."

"I'm serious. I don't have any other explanation for this physical reaction. We need to go. Stat."

"Why?" Before I can answer, he adds, "And you do know that we left a trail of popcorn." He looks down the hallway. "Stan can find us."

"Cory!" I snap. "Didn't they teach you at K-POP band camp that you don't ask questions? Read the room." I hold his face in between both of my hands and force the eye contact. He is inches from my face. "Read. The. Room."

"I'll get my things," Cory says quickly. *Good response, Cory.* He understands the assignment now. Before he disappears around the corner, he shouts back at me, "And they don't call it band camp. It's called a trainee program!"

With Cory gone, I am now without a shield from a potential Stan encounter. The risk of seeing Stan is still too high. I slowly back into the breakroom. I remain facing the hallway as I continue to diligently scan for Stan.

"Hi, Mary. Good evening," I say almost instinctively. I didn't bother to look behind me to see if Mary is actually there. I just assume she is. Sure enough, she responds.

"Hi, Sue," she says in her usual cheery tone. I am not surprised to hear her voice; I knew she would be in here. You can count on Mary to always be in the office before and after everyone else. One day, I should talk to her about how her unwavering loyalty to work will affect her health. But now is clearly not the time for that conversation.

With my back still facing Mary, I hang onto the door frame as I pop my head in and out of the hallway. I can sense Mary's confusion as she stands behind me watching my awkward movements. But again, now is not a good time. I cannot entertain her questions. I must quickly maneuver a stealthy, inconspicuous exit.

Cory rejoins me in the breakroom, and I grab onto his arm like a life raft. The death grip returns. I successfully use his body to hide myself for the last ten feet towards the exit door.

We make it outside and the fresh air provides much needed relief.

I finally let go of Cory's arm. He shakes his arm in relief as if I really hurt him. Maybe I did. Survival mode can bring upon unprecedented strength.

"Thanks," I say to Cory.

He looks at me with concerned eyes, but he doesn't pursue it further. "See you tomorrow," he simply says and begins to walk away from me. He doesn't take more than two steps before turning back around. "You owe me a bag of popcorn."

And off he goes.

I understand if my behavior in the last fifteen minutes seems unbecoming of an adult human. Some might say it was even an overreaction to nothing. My rebuttal is that I never felt such an overwhelming (almost suffocating) feeling as when I was alone in that conference room with Stan. Fight-or-flight mode kicked in. My brain picked flight. I ran away, as I do for almost all conflicts, big or small.

Moments. Moments make up the stories we retell. That single instance in the conference room with Stan will be a moment that stays with me. Whatever that was, I couldn't shake the feeling. It was the most unexpected, disruptive five seconds of my life. Five seconds of my life that cannot be undone. I'm confused why Stan, of all people, is the person who caused this moment to transpire. I am even less prepared to find out why the next day.

CHAPTER 7

Today is a new day. If you think that I am able to process my emotions and be better prepared to address them by now, you are unfortunately mistaken. A better person will walk head high into work and be able to have a mature, professional discussion with their boss about what unfolded last night. I, on the other hand, am a much lesser person.

The way I escaped work last night is how I plan on riding out this day. I just need to be in full ninja mode, on high alert, until I can find refuge in the glorious weekend ahead. I can do this. It can't be that hard to avoid my boss for the next eight hours.

Stan is waiting for me at my cubicle. Well, there goes my plan.

I see him leaning against my desk with his hands in his pockets. I notice he didn't take off his baseball cap, yet. His posture, along with those downturned eyes, reminds me of a child waiting for a ride that is uncomfortably late. I don't know what version of Stan I'll get today, but something is obviously off with this one, and I'm sure I have something to do with that.

He sees me approaching and straightens up. I'm greeted with immediate direct eye contact. Brown. His eyes are brown. A very light brown. I'm fixating on this arbitrary detail of his face to keep my pulse from racing.

Unfortunately, it's not working.

"Can I talk to you in my office?" Stan asks softly.

I should have had a better game plan for today; being a stealthy ninja is not in my wheelhouse. Stan has me cornered before I even get the chance to turn on my laptop this morning.

I follow him into his office. He closes the door behind me. There is no escaping this uncomfortable conversation now. He turns around to face me and I see the stress lines around his eyes. I can hear my own heart ticking as my breathing becomes shallow.

Brown. His eyes are light brown!

No, it's still not working.

He takes off his baseball cap, the same one he wears every day, and tosses it on his desk. Like clockwork, he runs his hand through his hair, but this time with a little more frustration than usual, as if he's mad about having such luxurious hair.

What was probably five seconds of silence felt like an eternity.

"Sue, I couldn't sleep at all last night," Stan says.

"Yes, that's a real problem. Herbal tea could have helped. Have you tried meditating? I slept so well last night," I say quickly, as if sentences didn't have periods. "I slept like a baby."

"I don't want to make you uncomfortable," he says. I must be radiating uneasiness, enough for him to sense it.

"I'm not uncomfortable. I am the *most* comfortable!"

"Clearly," he quips. He takes one step closer to me and those gentle eyes reappear just like that. He wears this look well, I admit.

I immediately feel a repeat of last night—that rush of uncontrollable adrenaline that stems from the unknown. It is not welcomed. This is all a little too much, too early in the morning.

Stan continues, "I want to address what happened last night."

I interject as if I have no manners. "You know, Stan, I realized that it's none of my business. I should not have asked those questions. I apologize if that made you uncomfortable. Let's just leave our personal lives out of the office and continue on as we were."

"Sue, you should know—"

There's a loud knock—more like a pounding—on the office door. Without waiting for a response, Michael enters. He speaks only three words. Nothing good ever comes after, "Conference room. Now."

Apparently, Stan and I didn't check our calendars this morning (too preoccupied, obviously). Michael scheduled a meeting at eight AM, which is exactly how I like to start my day. (That was sarcasm, by the way, in case it didn't translate well into writing).

Stan and I missed the memo.

We walk into a packed conference room; both Stan's and Michael's team are present. What kind of storm are we walking into? I'm betting that it's the smelly kind.

We take our seats and Michael immediately begins.

"We thought we had one of the biggest revenue generating opportunities of the year," Michael says as he paces the front of the room. "Based on Sue's report."

I do not like how he emphasized my name when he said it.

Michael looks directly at me and says, "Corporate shot it down." He then faces Stan. "It was riddled with mistakes."

"I thought your team checked it before it was sent out," Stan says.

"Regardless, the overhead didn't make sense; it's too high," Michael replies, ignoring Stan's question. "This should have been a red flag from the beginning. This kind of proposal should never have gone out. It's embarrassing that it did."

Utter confusion sets in. Is this the same Michael that asked me to join his team just a week earlier? This is the same person who praised my work and is now telling me that I "embarrassed" the team in front of, well, the entire team? I feel my blood boil. A private conversation would have conveyed the same message, but why is Michael making this such a public affair?

"Sue, this is a bad reflection on your performance. Stan, I don't know how you could stand behind these figures," Michael continues.

I am shocked and angry that Michael is still going at it. He looks ridiculous huffing and puffing in front of the team.

Michael, with all of his charisma and movie-star looks, has one serious flaw. I figured it out as I watched this scene unfold (a very unnecessary scene, at that). It is his narcissism, which needs to be fed constantly to cover up his insecurities. Today, he found a weakness and he pounced (to cover his own ass). Michael always has an agenda. He is deliberately putting on this show because people will talk after this—in his favor, he hopes.

All of my respect for him completely vanished. I can't believe that, at one point, I was in awe of him. And now with admiration lost, I am not going to allow myself to be disrespected by this overly ambitious man-child.

Stan gets up slowly from his seat, as if he's carrying a heavy load. I can feel the anger emitting off him.

"If you have a problem with anyone on my team, you talk to me directly," Stan says sternly. "You will not talk to Sue, or anyone on my team, in that manner."

Admiration lost on one hand is immediately gained by Stan on another. I admit that he won major points for having my back, but I am running on adrenaline, and I need to be heard.

I place my hand on Stan's arm. It snaps him out of his state of anger, and I can feel his body immediately relax.

"Please don't talk about my performance without looking at your own," I say directly to Michael. "If this is a poor reflection of me, it's worse of you. Where were you when we worked all day, into the night, for the past four nights?"

Michael looks surprised. The awkward, nervous girl that he usually encounters is not the person speaking to him now.

He looks even more surprised when I stand up to meet his eyes. Mr. Egotist will get all my attention and energy in the worst way. The things that I need to say, need to be said up close and personal. I am livid. I need to see him cringe. I don't care if there is an audience present to witness it.

"Where were *you*, Michael?" I ask again. "How long did you review the report before you stamped your name all over it and sent it up the chain? I can see why you're upset. It looks like you failed at doing your job."

I can't believe the words that are coming out of my mouth, much less the coherent manner in which I'm saying them. I unlocked a version of me that I didn't know I had. I guess anger *can* be useful (sometimes).

"You want to talk about overhead? Let's talk about overhead." Apparently, I have more to say. "What is your role? To catch mistakes? Our team works hard so that your job is easy. You haven't sent back a report in the last six years that I've worked here! Your job is redundant! If this company is really concerned about overhead, I'd start looking where you're standing."

I need to take a breather. My heart is pumping so fast that the room is starting to spin. But I am not done with him, yet.

I go on to say, "And the nerve to call a meeting with all these people present to chastise me is not only unprofessional, but a complete waste of everyone's time. Think of the number of employees sitting in this room right now and how they could be working on something more productive instead of listening to this nonsense!" *Am I done now? I think so.*

I can feel my old self resurfacing and freaking out at this new, bold me. When the room finally stops spinning, the silence follows, and it is deafening. I finally understand how silence can be so noisy. Empty airspace fills the room, and I can feel its weight push up against me.

I realize that I have not taken my eyes off of Michael the entire time; and now, I'm painfully aware that all the others in the room have their eyes on me. My old self has fully reemerged, and I am now paralyzed by self-consciousness.

The silence is disrupted by the sound of a slow clap coming from the back of the room. Of course, it is Cory. He stands up and looks at me with the biggest smile on his face.

"Now, *that* was excitement! I knew you had a wider range of emotions. Sue, you are not dead inside!" Cory exclaims as he looks at me proudly. The slow clapping is still going. I wish he would stop, but he is committed to cheering me on.

I lost count of how many times Cory has been my saving grace in my moments of vulnerability (or, in this case, my moment of complete and utter embarrassment). Of course, no one else joins in on the clapping, but my biggest advocate continues to stand proudly.

In times like these, when I desperately want to be anywhere else but here, there is only one thing left to do.

I turn to Stan and say, "I'm taking a mental health day." Or, in other words, I'm taking time to do some day-drinking.

Stan, of course, nods (not to grant permission, but to acknowledge that my message is received). I head towards the door.

"Me too!" I hear from behind me. You guessed it—it's Cory.

I give him a nod and we both get up to leave the conference room and the stunned audience within it.

The door clicks close behind me and I finally gasp for air. I may have displayed confidence on my way out, but I'm almost certain I'm going to be fired.

Confidence has consequences.

CHAPTER 8

I can't undo what I said, which was done in a conference room full of witnesses, but I can try to temporarily forget that I said it.

It's time to drink.

My last debacle with Michael was when my awkwardness kept me from saying anything; this latest debacle was when my anger made me say too much.

It's amazing how someone's position in my internal rankings can be so fragile. In one moment, Michael was up there as the untouchable man of class; in the next, he became small and pitiful. How quickly the mighty has fallen.

Cory, who seemingly has appointed himself as my new best friend, is right by my side as we march down this long hallway towards my favorite location in the building: the exit.

The exit, as usual, is near the breakroom. It's comforting that some things in life never change—like the location of my favorite door in this entire office (big caveat: it's only a favorite depending on which side of it I stand).

We pass the breakroom and I see Mary making coffee. It's probably the third carafe of the day.

I cannot explain why I did what I did next.

"Hey, Mary," I say as I poke my head inside the breakroom. "Do you want to take the rest of the day off and go do some early social drinking?" I added "social" in there because I thought it might appeal to her (and make this behavior seem a little less problematic).

Mary hesitates for a brief moment. It's not because she doesn't want to go; it's because she is taken aback that I'm even making this suggestion.

"Yes. Sure!" Mary responds happily.

As I mentioned before, I don't know what compelled me to ask Mary to join us, but I'm delighted that she agreed.

At this point, I think I should give you more insight into Mary; however, I don't have that much to share about her. She's been at this company longer than I have and she loves this place (as I think I've emphasized enough by now). Mary seems like a genuinely happy person. If I stop to really think about it, I realize that we both work at a job that—for lack of a better word—sucks. It does. There's no need for me to sugarcoat it. The traditional corporate job sucks; not so much because of the actual work itself as much as the behavior that manifests in this kind of setting. The gossiping, the backstabbing, the brownnosing, the relentless pursuit of recognition—these are all the things that this culture breeds. How are we supposed to be better versions of ourselves if, for eight hours out of the day, we are immersed in this kind of toxicity? Well, you can be like me and dread every moment spent in this living hell; or be like Mary and embrace the good parts.

I don't know much about Mary, but I do know that she has an unwavering ability to be positive and consistently kind. You will never catch Mary rolling her eyes in annoyance or making a snide comment about anyone. Not once. Mary has no bad days. If she does, she diminishes it into a bad moment and then moves on. She's just here, and she's happy. It's remarkable.

Perhaps I subconsciously need to be around this kind of human. I just had an encounter with one of the bad ones, and I need to believe that our species can do better. Mary is better.

In fact, Mary turned out to be better than better.

Happy hour starts out as awkwardly as one might expect. I'm here with one coworker who I barely spoke to before now, and another who seems strangely too familiar in the short amount of time that I've known him. This makes for an odd three-person dynamic, but here we are.

A few drinks in and some truths come out.

Cory, being the young, hip one in our trio, tells us about his travel adventures after college, which he documented on social media. He apparently is a big deal on one of those social media apps with over 100,000 followers. Mary and I barely have five friends combined, so you can imagine how thoroughly impressed we are.

We also learned that Cory comes from a well-to-do family. *Very* well-to-do. I usually reserve a small amount of disdain for the rich because I imagine they go through life thinking it's okay to poo-poo on others. However, Cory grew on me even more after this revelation because I would have never pegged him as wealthy. He doesn't present himself as such, and that is how I like the rich: indistinguishable (at least on the surface) amongst the masses.

And then there is Mary's truth. Mary's husband died from cancer almost a decade ago. It was a five-year battle that he lost. They have been together since their teens. To further the tragedy, her parents died in a car accident shortly after her husband passed. Mary was on her way to meet them for dinner, but they never showed up at the restaurant. (I know, it sounds like a plot to a sad movie with no ending). To add to her unfortunate circumstance, Mary is an only child and never had children of her own; not because she didn't want to, but because she couldn't. So, she has been a family of one ever since that day (her exact words).

All of this information is shared as if it is a short story she's told over and over again. It seems immensely unfair that such unfortunate events can happen to the same person in a single lifetime. Cory and I sit in awe as we listen to every word. As she reveals these tragic details about her life, Mary is still emitting this unparalleled aura of positivity.

Is this what inner peace looks like? I envy it. I want it.

Mary's resilience is admirable; some people are just built (or conditioned) differently—*stronger*. All of these years, I simply wrote her off as the office busybody with nothing better to do. But in fact, she is the one true badass amongst us all. She is better than most. I know that her type will keep our species from devolving into heathens.

"Mary," I say as seriously as I can, "you just made me believe in humanity again. How are you not angry and bitter all the time?"

"I was for a while," Mary replies. "Everything made me angry. When it rained, I got angry. When I ran out of milk, I got angry, and I don't even like milk. *Everything* made me upset."

"How did you make it stop?" Cory asks.

"I chose to change. It didn't happen overnight, of course. I just couldn't keep living that way. So, every day I practiced being happier. Some days I faked it but *acting* happier actually made me *feel* happier. Then I found little things that I would enjoy, and I just focused on those things more intensely than others. Like how to make a superior cup of coffee."

"That sounds like a lot of work," I say unenthusiastically.

"Making coffee or being happy?" she asks.

"Both."

"It was a lot of work—trying to be happy, that is. And it's still a lot of work, but I learned so much about myself and other people. I like to observe people…as you probably already know. Talking to people, seeing what makes others happy helped me relearn that there is so much more left to life."

Mary stops to finish off her beer. She surprisingly asks for another one immediately. Cory and I can't let our elders drink us under the table, so we do the same. A round for everyone.

"For example," Mary continues, "my neighbor loves butterflies as if he sees them for the first time, every time. He stops and watches them, then goes on with his day with the biggest smile on his face. I have no idea what his other interests are, but I do know that the man loves butterflies."

"Who doesn't though?" Cory asks rhetorically. "Even pedophiles love butterflies."

Mary guffaws. I don't think I ever heard such a loud noise escape such a tiny woman.

"That isn't the point!" she says gleefully. After Mary contains herself, she gives me a serious look and says, "And then there's Stan, your boss."

I stop. Hearing his name just now made my stomach drop. I try my best to keep the internal emotional turmoil from surfacing onto my face. Cory sees it though, almost immediately. His smile fades as he studies my face.

"What about him?" I ask as indifferently as I can. "Stan loves working more than anything."

Mary gently smiles at me. I knew straight away, judging by the way she looked at me, that she was going to tell me something I wasn't ready to hear.

"Sue, you should hear the way he talks about you when you're not in the room."

"I'm a reliable worker. He's lucky to have me on his team," I reply, trying to divert the direction of this conversation. I do not like where this is going.

"You know what I mean," Mary says.

"I don't, actually. I'm not certain of many things these days. I don't understand people most of the time, so I try not to assume too much but when I do, you won't believe how many times my assumptions have been proven wrong—just this week alone." I don't take a single breath as I provide that unprompted response. "I don't really like people"—I look around the table—"current company excluded."

Both Cory and Mary laugh, or at least, they are humoring me.

"You shouldn't give yourself too much credit," Cory says. "You are not that big of a cynic as you think you are."

And just then, as if it was due to some transcendent cosmic timing, Paul, my almost ex-fiancé, walks into the bar. I know that sounds like the beginning of a joke, and unfortunately, I'm probably at the butt of this one.

He sees me. I know he did. We, in fact, lock eyes. But he does not acknowledge me; much less, come over to greet me. I cannot blame him, but I expected us to be cordial at the very least. We were together for four years and friends for even longer. Again, I don't understand people.

I feel Cory's eyes on me as I stare at the back of Paul's head. Paul finally disappears from my view.

I turn to Cory and say, "Love lost." After a moment, I correct myself. "Maybe not love. But something was lost."

All that Cory says in response is, "He looks rich. You should have married him."

I laugh so hard that beer comes out of my nose. The sight of this (a wonderful imagery, I'm sure) causes Mary to do the same. Beer everywhere.

"Oh my god! How drunk are you two?" Cory exclaims.

There are some people who are meant to be in your life. You can try to push them away—shun them even—but somehow, a few will break through your walls and become your center. These two at the bar, Cory and Mary, have momentarily alleviated my chronic allergy to people. Despite my recent emotional whirlwind, I find happiness in the company at present.

I wish I knew this would be the last time we would laugh together before it all abruptly came to an end.

CHAPTER 9

Mary did not show up for work on Monday morning. I hope she is playing hooky. That woman needs a break from this place. The weekend, those measly two days, is not enough time to make one miss the office. I wish I was playing hooky with Mary right now. Perhaps it's not too late.

Then I look over at my desk. Reality sinks in; it *is* too late. I already turned on my computer, and half the office saw me walking in this morning. I am stuck here for the day.

On a positive note, I have successfully not made contact with any managers yet, Stan and Michael specifically. I'm trying my best to keep a low profile today. I might even limit the number of times I go to the bathroom to minimize the chances of someone stopping me in the hallway. Obligatory human interaction is not what I want today (or on most days). The three and a half walls of my cubicle serve as my only shield, and I plan on staying within them.

But, of course, my plans to lay low are immediately ruined.

I hear commotion coming from Michael's office. It's loud. Noticeably loud. It's not exactly at yelling level, but it's uncomfortable enough to start some office murmur.

I keep my head down. I want no part of this. Then I hear Stan's voice overlapping with Michael's. His voice is like a beacon; I immediately get up and walk towards it.

I know that I shouldn't have. I should have just put on my headphones and blasted some Beyoncé (because Queen Bey can motivate me to do anything—even work). But no, here I am lurking outside of Michael's office. I strain my neck by extending it as far as it could go as I try to listen in. I don't know why I think the extra half centimeter of neck distance will help me hear their conversation any better. Sometimes logic escapes me.

"What are you doing?" A voice startles me from behind.

Of course, it is Cory. By now, it's a pattern that this kid just appears at the most inopportune times. Or, maybe they are the most opportune times. The distinction between the two is usually not realized until after the fact.

"Exactly what it looks like," I whisper. "Now hush."

"They are probably talking about you," he whispers back.

"Why would you say that? As if I'm not stressed out enough. Do you think I'm getting fired?"

Cory forces a smile, the kind that has trouble brewing behind it. "Let's find out."

Without hesitation, he opens the office door. The nerve this kid has is almost admirable. I emphasize "almost."

I stay behind, but Cory gently grabs my wrist and leads me into the room. I'll need to have a talk with him later about how life isn't a Korean drama, and how he should never grab me without expecting a punch to the face. But now is not the time.

I'm suddenly standing in a room of people with whom I didn't want to share the air. Serves me right. I had the choice to listen to Beyoncé, but instead I ended up here. What was I thinking? *Always choose Beyoncé. Always!*

Michael and Stan are surprised by our presence as we enter the room uninvited. Go figure.

"Get out." Michael says bluntly.

"That sounds good to me!" I exclaim, grabbing Cory's arm as I walk back towards where we entered. However, Cory doesn't budge.

"You guys are very loud," Cory says matter-of-factly. "Everyone can hear you outside. And you're making her uncomfortable." He points at me, as if he couldn't be any clearer about who he's referring to.

I put on my best opposing face. "What? No, I'm not uncomfortable," I say as I inadvertently blow raspberries. Biggest lie I told today.

"Regardless. It's very unprofessional," he continues in a rather professional tone. Then he simply walks out of the room, and I watch him leave.

Yes, that just happened—he simply walked out. He really left me. *Thanks, Cory.* He's usually one to save me from these situations, but today he walked me directly into one.

Something is off with him. The big giveaway is that he's wearing a suit today. It's the kind of suit that young people pair with sneakers. Professional, yet casual, all at the same time.

Something is definitely off.

We all watch in silence as Cory closes the door behind him. As soon as the door clicks close, Michael turns to face Stan (as if I'm not in the room). "You need to keep your direct reports in line," Michael says to Stan, although it is clearly apparent that he's saying it for me to hear.

"He's not one of mine," Stan says.

They both turn to me. I now have their unwanted attention. I simply shrug. Whatever chaos was brewing in this office before is now replaced by confusion. If Cory is not on Stan's team, and he's not on Michael's, who does he report into?

We all turn and look towards the door where Cory exited just moments earlier. After a minute of silence, I ask the question that we are collectively thinking. "What does he do here?"

CHAPTER 10

I left Michael's office in a hurry. I didn't bother to excuse myself; I just left. I shouldn't have been there in the first place.

I try to make a beeline to my cubicle, but I'm stopped by John. You remember John, right? Guy who takes forever to do his job, guy who gets paid more than me, guy who caused the virus outbreak on our entire network. Him. He stopped me on my mission to get back to my desk and I wasn't thrilled by his interruption. Not one single cell in my body wants to be anywhere near John today, but the Universe has other plans (as it usually does).

John dives right in. "So, is it true?" he asks. He assumes I know what he's talking about.

"What are you referring to?" I ask as I try to bury my annoyance deep down inside of me. It is an exercise that takes a lot of energy and patience.

"Is Michael getting fired? You were just in his office."

"Why would he get fired?" I am now begrudgingly invested in this conversation. I want to know more. This is a rare occasion in which I willingly pursue a conversation with John. *Do tell.*

John goes on to inform me that someone talked to human resources about Michael's stint last week. Apparently, many were unimpressed by what they witnessed in that conference room. One person in particular (who remains anonymous), was so appalled by Michael's behavior that they decided to report it. Could this be the reason for the commotion in Michael's office this morning? Was Stan the one that reported him?

I then decide to stop my short and poorly executed investigation into this Stan-and-Michael matter. I am no longer invested. I must focus on my new mission: find Cory.

It wasn't hard to find him at all. My mission is quickly completed when I see him leaning against my desk. It looks like he's been waiting for me to come out of Michael's office this entire time.

"You!" I angrily say to him.

He puts up his hands in surrender. "I know, I know. But you needed to know. Were they fighting about you? Are you going to be fired? Just find out and move on. There's no point in dragging out the agony of wondering about it for the rest of the day."

Yet again, I cannot argue with his logic. Is everyone in his generation born with some kind of life navigation? I surely don't remember having one at his age.

Cory takes a deep breath in and exhales. "Let's both try to get through this day without any more drama," he says.

Yes, there is definitely something off about him today. He seems *almost* stressed. Actually, I'm not quite sure what this look on his face really means. This is a new side of Cory I have yet to see. My desire to karate chop him for taking me into Michael's office earlier has now dissipated completely. Something is weighing on him. I cannot kick him while he's carrying a heavy load. I'll do it later.

Not before long, John makes an unwelcomed second appearance. He rushes by us and whispers, "CEO incoming. Headed this way. Disappear. Now." And then he was gone. He took his own advice and disappeared. Why do people like John get so nervous around upper management? Then I remember that it's John, after all. If I was that incompetent at my job, I would be afraid of being exposed too.

Before I could scatter like the rest of the office mice, I spot our CEO about a few yards away.

I'll take a pause here from my current drama to say this: in an environment made up of mostly white male middle managers, it's a breath of fresh air to see this five-foot-two Asian woman—I repeat: ASIAN WOMAN—walk down this hallway and is so clearly capable of conjuring up self-doubt and insecurities within seemingly competent adults. I love it, but I will also do my best to bury all signs of weakness while in her presence.

I quickly turn to Cory and whisper, "Pretend to work!"
He gives me deadpan eyes. He is clearly unmoved.

Then I remember why I rushed to find Cory in the first place. It wasn't only to cause him physical harm for pulling me into Michael's office; no, it was also to ask him who is his boss since neither Stan nor Michael claims him as one of theirs.

Two words later, I get my answer.

CHAPTER 11

H i, Mom," Cory says quietly to Angela Lee, the CEO of the company. I did an immediate double take at Cory and then at the woman whom he just addressed as "mom" at our place of work.

It took me a half second too long to realize the nature of their relationship. The "mom" part was a huge giveaway, but I failed to register what it meant immediately. Cory *Lee*. We work at Analytic-*Lee* (yes, that's a play on words). Lee is a fairly common last name around here, so I never made the connection. Moreover, I would have never suspected that my new bestie at work is related to the CEO, much less her actual offspring. I knew he came from a well-off family, but I assumed his money came from a successful boba shop (or two), not from a large private corporation specializing in data analytics for major U.S. retailers. I clearly underestimated his wealth (and revealed some personal biases).

I understand now why Cory seemed a little off today. He knew that Angela Lee would come to the office on this day, and he owes me a big explanation. Or does he? It's not like I shared with him all of my familial ties, or favorite color, or medical history. To be fair, he doesn't owe me anything, right?

At the very least, he knew an awkward conversation with me is in the near future once his family tree becomes known around the office. Well, it is now known. We should talk about it.

But before I can pursue that, Cory pleadingly gives me a "not now" look. I hold his stare for a little longer than usual and then I give him a slight nod. We can unpack all of this later; right now, he looks like he needs to talk to his mommy. Yes, I said "mommy" purely for effect. I couldn't help it.

I watch as Cory walks off with his CEO mother. I've wondered how the other side lived. What kind of children do the filthy rich raise? Apparently, they are capable of rearing some pretty good ones. I admire Angela Lee even more than before, now that I know she produced a human like Cory.

I've had enough excitement for the rest of the year. I should glue myself to my desk and get some work done now. Working will help the time pass faster.

It's now 8:56 AM. Countdown to lunchtime begins. I am already starving. I put on my headphones and get to work.

I must have worked for what felt like two hours straight. And then I look up at the oversized wall clock and it's only 9:30 AM. What a disappointment. I feel dejected that I cannot push the day to move any faster.

Time is moving slowly today, and then it completely stops when the Universe sends me Stan.

"Congratulations, Sue. You got promoted," Stan says in the least congratulatory tone possible. He said it as if he's reading me the lunch specials. He sees I'm clearly confused and proceeds to explain. "You got the spot on Michael's team. Effective immediately."

Stan abruptly ends our conversation and walks away. I get up to go after him. He does not slow down, so now we are walking and talking. I'm already out of breath as I try to match his pace.

"I didn't apply for the position. I don't want the position," I tell him.

"Consider it an involuntary transfer with a pay raise," Stan says. Again, the deadpan tone. He still does not slow down his pace, much less look at me.

"You're not listening. I don't want to go to Michael's team. I'm happy where I am."

Stan abruptly turns around, so quickly that I walk right into him. We stand face to face (well, more like face to chest as he hovers over me).

"It's a promotion, Sue. Accept it. Be happy about it. You deserve it." The dissonance between his words and his tone could not be more jarring.

He walks into his office and closes the door in front of me. Well, that is the end of that.

I should be elated to hear those words coming out of his mouth. I work really hard (maybe not *that* hard, but I work smart). I *do* deserve a promotion. What would normally be happy news is overshadowed by the delivery of it.

The truth is, his coldness is bothering me more than I'm used to. It pains me to see this version of Stan.

Of course, I then hear the wise words of Cory Lee in my head: "Don't drag out the agony." He's right. There's really no point in doing that. I do not want to go the rest of the day feeling the way I'm feeling. So, I will take this newly given advice from a kid and go be an adult right now.

I take a deep breath and convince myself to proceed.

I open the door to Stan's office. He's sitting behind his desk hunched over. His head is in his hands. I recognize the posture of a defeated man when I see it.

"What is your problem?" I say rather unexpectedly. I didn't know what exactly I was going to say to him, but I thought it might be something a little less aggressive than that.

He looks up at me. As soon as our eyes meet, I immediately knew that I should not have walked into this room in the first place. Have you ever had that feeling? It's called instant regret. This was a mistake. I should have just let this man be.

The look he wears now reminds me of that night in the conference room. I can deal with Stan when he is short with me. I can deal with him when he's too bossy or too stressed. I know that version of him all too well. I've known that version for the past six years. However, this man before me now seems broken and sad. I don't have an instruction manual for this version of Stan.

I approach his desk. He doesn't move. In a gentler tone, I ask, "What did I do to you?"

His face instantly changes. The wrinkle between his eyebrows disappears and his eyes soften. He replies, "You have no idea, do you?"

I cannot move in this moment as his eyes hold mine captive. I'm too afraid my breathing would disrupt the momentary peace between us. I'm holding onto the silence as if it's the only thing holding me up right now. I can feel the blood pumping throughout my entire being as I wait for the next few moments to unfold.

The truth is, I *do* have an idea, one that I didn't want to unpack. However, judging by my current predicament, it looks like I will have to do so.

Here it goes.

* * *

I've worked for Stan ever since I started here at Analytic-Lee. He hired me after we met at a conference about new data mining technology. (In case you haven't already pegged me as a nerd, then that should do it). Yes, we met at a data analytics convention. It was amazing! I was chatting it up (which is not my default), but I was young then and anxious to excel at my future career. I believe this practice is what you might call "networking." I networked. I networked myself into an interview with Stan and he hired me.

I've always admired Stan. Admiration should not be confused with attraction, however. I admire his strict work ethic and even his robotic-like composure in almost all settings (he is consistent). As short as he can be at times, he's never yelled at or minimized me when he's having a bad day (and I've witnessed many of his bad days). I have studied him for the past six years and the one thing I know for sure about this man is that work is his hobby. I cannot read him most times, but I know his priorities. Work comes first. Whatever comes after that, he keeps as a mystery. And *that* is why I never found myself attracted to Stan.

Physically? Sure, he passes the bar. I have eyes, after all. That aside, if someone doesn't open up to you, it's hard to strike up any romantic feelings—the opportunity just isn't there to do so. I don't know Stan. I've gone this long without really knowing him and I have gone this long without feeling anything for him.

Up until recently, I thought our feelings of nothingness toward each other were mutual. And now? Looking at this man before me, I can see that I was wrong. I am not one to think that I could ever bring a man to his knees, but I'm self-aware enough to know that I've affected Stan in a way that I never thought I could.

To be fair to him, I need to acknowledge it. *Enough running away, Sue. Be an adult and deal with adult feelings, as uncomfortable as they may be.*

It's time to let him say what he needs to say.

* * *

As I unpacked all of this in my mind, I must have been staring off into the distance. I didn't notice that Stan had moved from his desk and is now within inches of me. I feel the warmth emanating off him as we stand in each other's breathing space. I can see the specks of gold in his brown eyes. I see the undeniable longingness in his stare.

"I don't like how Michael poached you—from me," Stan says just slightly above a whisper. It's the "from me" part that sent a shiver down my spine. It subtly carries weight. I could have easily ignored it if not for the wistful look in his eyes.

"Was that the argument between you two this morning?" I'm stalling. I no longer care what that argument was about. I'm delaying the part where he tells me what his eyes are really trying to say.

He shrugs. It seems like he doesn't care about that argument anymore either. "I cannot protect you now that you're on Michael's team," he says.

"I don't need to be protected. That man's ego is quite fragile. I know where to hit him if I must." Again, stalling.

He nods. He knows I'm right. And then, unprompted, he says, "I'm sad to see you go. Truth is, I don't want you to go."

It takes a moment for those words to sink in. This is the closest Stan has ever expressed any feelings—good or bad—towards me. When I got hired for his team, he shook my hand and told me to "do well." When my birthday comes around, he signs my card with "-Stan." Look how far we've come. It only took six years for any fragment of good feelings to culminate in that last sentence he just spoke to me. This is groundbreaking.

I suppose this would be a good time to offer a response—something, anything—but instead, I let the silence sub for words.

His eyes tell me that there's more for him to say, yet his lips remain still.

He moves in closer. *Or did I imagine that?*

I suddenly find it difficult to move.

I can hear his breathing clearer now. Yes, I can confirm that he is, indeed, closer to my face than he was a few seconds ago. I start to panic. What do I do? We are so close that I can count every blemish on his face (there aren't that many).

He reaches for something behind me and reveals a small, wrapped package. Am I relieved that he was not going in for a kiss? Or am I disappointed? My body tells me it's a little bit of both.

"A parting gift," he says. "Nothing fancy. Just a notebook with the words, 'This meeting could have been an email,' inscribed on the cover."

He knows me well, apparently.

"Good luck with Michael." His facial expression switches back and forth between wistful and sad, and now he seamlessly blends the two.

I look at the gift in my hands. How did he know that my humor is usually the anti-corporate-work kind? I'm moved. I continue to stare at the gift as if it's the most fragile thing I've ever held in my hands (as if it's not just a bunch of paper bounded together and slapped with the customary high markup). I tell myself that it's only a notebook; however, this gift is everything right now.

I should tell him that. I should tell him how much I love this simple gesture; how perfect a gift this is for someone like me. It's beyond thoughtful.

But instead, I say, "You should have paid me more." I try to keep a serious expression, but I immediately break.

We both burst out laughing. It's the kind of laughter that is followed by tears, an indication that there's a lot to unpack here.

I am not that funny to trigger such a response. However, the laughter and tears seem like the most appropriate vessels to channel these haywire feelings.

I need to hold myself up as my stomach starts to hurt from laughing and crying so passionately from my gut. He instinctively pulls me in and wraps his arms around my head, which is now leaning against his chest. I know this doesn't sound romantic in written form—at all—but it's endearing, I promise you. It's a natural progression of our body language as we both recover from laughing and crying.

I embrace his embrace. This is weirdly comforting, but it ends abruptly.

The door to Stan's office opens.

"What is going on here?"

CHAPTER 12

Stan and I look over towards the sound of the voice. Instinctively, we take a step away from each other without taking our eyes off of the person standing in the doorway.

Cory stands there with his hands in his pockets and he rocks back and forth on his heels. His eyes bewilderedly dart back and forth between Stan and me.

"Okay, so this is awkward," Cory says. "I'm going to be very honest here. I'm uncomfortable with all of this." He gestures at Stan and I together. "Let's just pretend I didn't witness whatever it was that I just witnessed."

"Sounds good!" I immediately say a little too enthusiastically.

I quickly glance over at Stan. His eyes are searching my face for answers as to what just happened here. I don't have any for him.

"See you later," I say to Stan. I add a brief wave of the hand at the end of that sentence. Needless to say, I am unimpressed with how I chose to make my exit. I might as well have given him a high five or a fist bump (don't worry, I did not).

As is common practice lately, I shuffle Cory towards the door. Once we are outside of Stan's office, he smiles coyly at me.

"We are going to unpack all of *that* later," he says quietly.

I immediately counter with, "Oh, there's a lot about today that we need to unpack, buddy."

He puts up both hands in defeat.

"But for now, let's go meet your new team!" he says, clearly faking enthusiasm.

"You heard?" I ask.

"Everyone heard. I don't think Michael is your biggest fan. Hence, the yelling match with Stan this morning."

I give him deadpan eyes. "I'm not exactly *his* either. I don't understand how this happened. If he doesn't want me on his team, why was I transferred?"

And there it is. I see it immediately. *It*. That look on Cory's face, like a kid caught stealing a cookie mid-steal. His eyes move around a little too much and a little too directly away from me.

"You little shit," I say as calmly and as quietly as I could. He cowers away from me. "I just found out—*today*—that you are the CEO's son, someone who can actually get every single person here fired, and now I find out that you are playing with my career in your tiny little baby hands? What gives?" I try to keep my tone as even-keeled as possible. "If you think you're doing me a favor, you're not. You're really, really not."

"First of all, you didn't need to exaggerate 'tiny little baby hands,'" he says as he puts up both hands for me to see. "They are fitting for a growing boy! Secondly, I didn't do it for you," he counters. "Well, I did, but it's for the better of the company. Michael's team is weak, Sue. You will make it stronger. I simply made a suggestion to people who agreed and who made it happen."

"'People'?" I ask. "Like your mom?"

"Her too." He nods matter-of-factly.

I give Cory my best unamused face as I stare directly into his eyes. "Who are you, Cory Lee? I liked you better yesterday."

I suddenly feel the weight of exhaustion on my shoulders. I've been running on adrenaline all morning. It's been an eventful Monday. I'm too tired to get worked up over my job transfer anymore. It's a promotion. I should accept it, even though it feels like defeat.

As soon as I think the excitement is over, I see Michael, my newly assigned boss, walking towards me with obvious purpose. I methodically scan my surroundings. I conclude that there is no good place to hide. Cory then gently squeezes my arm; it snaps me out of my minor panic, and I put on my best smile at the incoming human wrecking ball. A quick flash of Miley Cyrus' music video comes to mind—you know the one.

Michael immediately gets to the point of his visit.

"I don't know who the hell thought it was a good idea to move you onto my team, but let me tell you something," Michael says as he moves inches closer to my face. "I don't tolerate insubordination. I know Stan goes easy on you. I'm not him. Are we clear?"

I feel myself shaking. I'm too tired to defend his verbal blows. Exhaustion makes me vulnerable.

Before I'm able to offer a reply to Michael, I notice that Cory immediately straightens his posture and widens his stance. He looks *almost* angry. This is another new look on him. I'm seeing all sides of Cory today.

"Is that a threat?" Cory asks Michael.

Up until now, Michael was squarely focused on me. He must not have noticed Cory standing there this entire time. Cory redirects Michael's attention onto himself. He looks ready to humble Michael, who, in truth, needs a lesson (or two) in modesty.

Cory continues, "You should be more careful throwing your weight around like that. Tact goes a long way."

"This is between me and her. Please move along."

I just realize that Michael still has no idea who Cory is. Word must not have traveled around as quickly as I thought it would.

This should be interesting.

Michael takes a closer look at Cory, as if he didn't bother to acknowledge who he was speaking to in the first place. Then he remembers. "*You* again. Why are you always just hanging around? Don't you have a job to do?"

Cory simply shrugs, as if that's an adequate response to the question. The audacity of the young! I admit that I admire it.

I'm in a trance watching these two stare at each other for seconds too long. It's uncomfortable now. I don't know who will win in this I'll-show-you-who's-alpha match.

Michael squints his eyes at Cory. "What do you do here?" He folds his arms across his chest as he waits for an answer.

"Maybe next time, we can sit down, and I will properly explain my role to you," Cory replies.

I couldn't help but smile at that. If only Michael knew the weight behind that statement.

The look on Michael's face tells me he was not expecting that kind of answer from Cory. I probably shouldn't antagonize my new boss, but it's a challenge to hide my amusement about this situation. I do my best, however, to contain my inner giggles. I will be a professional and I will bury this joy deep, *deep* down inside where it can never see the light of this workplace.

Cory gives me a wink. He's clearly amused too.

Michael's eyes bounce back and forth between Cory and me. He, for one, is clearly *not* amused. He seems confused by our disposition (and I don't blame him). We are giving off a weird energy; albeit it's fitting considering the day we're both having.

I woke up today thinking it'll be another Mundane Monday. However, so much has happened today—and it's not even lunchtime yet!

If I said I was exhausted before, I'm dying now. It's been too long since I've eaten. I shuffle Cory to the nearest exit (this is our routine now, it seems). We leave Michael in his state of confusion. I am not so secretly reveling in Michael's current predicament.

Lunchtime should provide some reprieve from all the unexpected events from this morning. Too much excitement can take a toll on the body.

"Don't expect me to buy your lunch from now on," Cory says while walking and looking down at his phone.

Of course, I would never expect him to pay, but we both know he can surely afford to do so.

All of a sudden, he looks up at me and his face has changed. The color is gone. His eyes are wide. "I just got an email from human resources," Cory says. "It's about Mary."

CHAPTER 13

Mary passed. I've had bad Monday mornings before, but this one takes it.

I'm going to fast forward a few weeks here. I'll save you the details of how everyone seemed shocked, yet indifferent, at the news of Mary's passing. The hard truth is that some people put on quite a sad face after hearing the news, and then they go about their day as usual in the seconds that follow. I suppose that's how it should be. Death happens. Life goes on. We are conditioned and obligated to show sympathy upon hearing bad news. I get it. Yet, somehow, those who feign sadness are the ones that trouble me, especially from where I am sitting now.

I chose to sit at the back of the funeral hall. As did Cory. We both watch in silence as the room fills with people, most of whom are people from work. It bothers me—deeply—that some chose to sit right up front. I don't know much about funeral etiquette, but I figure those seats are reserved for family members of the deceased. Albeit Mary has no family but those who chose the front row didn't know that. In fact, most of the office didn't know Mary at all. In the years that she's been with the company, I have not seen any of these people sit with her at lunch, or exchange anything more than short pleasantries during their breakroom encounters. And yet, here they are—front and center at Mary's funeral. Some people just don't understand they are not the main character in every setting.

I feel sick.

Cory notices something's wrong. His concerned eyes try to read the situation. I gesture to him that I'll be alright. However, seconds later, I feel the need to vomit. Is this a physical manifestation of all my emotions, which have seemingly accumulated into a pile of bricks in my stomach? I think it is.

I can feel someone taking a seat to my right as I'm hunched over my knees in an attempt to control the nausea. I slowly sit back up and I'm greeted by my new adjacent chairmate.

It's Stan. He whispers, "Are you alright?"

Those eyes. There are stories abound in those worrisome eyes, stories that have yet to be told. I catch myself staring into his eyes for a little too long, so much so that I momentarily forget that I'm sick to my stomach. The flashback of our embrace takes over my headspace—vividly. I'm looking directly at Stan's face but the image of us in his office is all that I can see.

He must have noticed that I'm lost in my thoughts. He looks away, but not before I catch the slight smile on his face.

I blush immediately.

Here I am at a funeral, and the emotions are not fitting for the current setting. I'm swinging back and forth on a pendulum of feelings. Again, I start to feel sick.

Cory nudges my arm and directs my attention to an elderly man who is quickly making a beeline towards us.

"Are you Sue?" he asks. "I've been asking around and the people up front pointed in your direction." He leans in closer to me. "Are you Sue?" he urgently asks again.

It took me too long to process what he's asking.

"She is," Cory answers for me.

"I'm so glad I found you! Listen, Mary might have mentioned that she has no next of kin. Would you kindly say a few words up there?" says this man with big pleading eyes and a toothy smile.

"You…are…her…neighbor," I say slowly instead of answering his question. Okay, my brain is finally catching up, making the connections now. Mary told us about her exuberant, elderly neighbor. This man in front of me fits the bill.

"Yes!" he exclaims. He's ecstatic that I knew that. "She must have talked about me too! She surely talked about you. She said she had one of the best times of her life with you. She mentioned a 'Sue' and another gentleman that I can't remember the name of." He pauses to conjure up a memory. He gives up trying and continues, "She just described him as a 'kind, beautiful boy.'"

"Cory?" I offer.

"Yes!" he exclaims again. His happiness explodes. "That's it!"

Cory raises his hand. "Boy. Here," he says.

"You! I can't believe I found you both!" the man shouts. He is gleaming. He practically jumps for joy, causing his glasses to slide down the bridge of his nose. He pushes his glasses up and gets a closer look at both Cory and me. After he studies our faces, he says in a rather serious tone, "You have no idea how happy she was after that night out. She said it was the best non-work workday she's ever had. Of course, she couldn't stop talking about her new friends from work."

My eyes start to well. Mary and I were practically strangers for the majority of the time that we've known each other. Then, we had just one night of swapping stories and sharing laughter, and that was enough to carve out a space in each other's lives. To state the obvious, all of us are strangers until we are simply not.

My mom used to tell me that quality time spent together is different from time spent together. I never found that quite profound. The poignancy of that saying may have been diluted when translated into broken English. Regardless, the sentiment is not lost on me as I sit on this pew. Mom was right. She was *so* right. With thoughts of my mom alongside thoughts of Mary, the floodgates open; the tears are now flowing.

The gleeful old man reaches out and places his hand over mine. "There is no need for the tears. This"—he looks around the room—"is life. And Mary made the best of hers. She would want us to revel the fact that her death brought us together. And there's probably a reason why this 'kind, beautiful boy' and"—he looks over at Stan whom he just now noticed—"this rather handsome fellow is sitting exactly where they are, right now in this moment, beside you."

I smile at this elderly man before me. His spirit is contagious.

"That's better. Now go on up there. Let's get this party going! After you're done, just give me a signal and I will release the butterflies," the man says with a smile that spreads from ear to ear.

I let out a laugh, despite my tears. I look over at Cory. I can tell by the look on his face that he remembers too. I gently squeeze his hand. He also realized that this elderly man is Mary's neighbor, the one who loves butterflies. She mentioned that very specific detail about him. Do you ever hear something about someone, and then when you finally meet them, it all seems to make sense? His love of butterflies makes sense.

I make my way to the front. My nausea is completely gone. From where I'm standing, I can see Stan and Cory stealing glances at each other. Somehow, they keep missing eye contact. One of them would look at the other while the other wasn't looking. Then, they take turns. It's quite an awkward game they're playing. I'm easily amused by it.

I see Mary's neighbor standing in the aisle. He holds his hands together, anxiously awaiting my signal so that he can release his beloved butterflies.

I see the familiar faces from the office in the front row. It's a small group of people that showed up for Mary's funeral. That made me terribly sad. Again, the pendulum of emotions continues to swing.

I'm reminded that anger can propel you forward with confidence. Oddly, sadness can do the same. I supposed it's less confidence and more I-don't-give-two-fucks-anymore. Slight difference. The normal me would choke standing in front of these people. But today, I just don't care what any of them think. It's not about me; it's not about them.

"Why do we gather to show that we care *after* one has passed?" I even surprised myself with that opening statement. I wasn't expecting to lead with that.

The funeral hall is dead silent. No pun intended.

"When she was alive, how many of us took the time to get to know her?" I ask. I can see some people shift uncomfortably in their seats. "I'll be honest. It took me six years too long to finally get past, 'Hi, how are you doing?' I can say this with confidence now: we—all of us—missed out on getting to know an amazing person. We are so trapped in our own micro universes, and we forget how beautiful it can be when we collide." Again, I surprised myself. That was rather unintentionally poetic. Sadness can tap into a different side of a person, apparently.

I'm not sure where to go from here. I pause and my eyes land on Stan and Cory. They are no longer awkwardly stealing glances at each other; their eyes are squarely on me.

"It pains me that I didn't get to know Mary sooner," I finally say. "Timing isn't always on my side, but the timing of Mary's passing is particularly cruel. We just recently became more than coworkers, more than just someone you pass in the hall. Now I'll never get the chance to hear the rest of her stories, which remain as forever untold stories. There's so much we don't know about those who we see practically every day. I think about the smiles we miss, or the pain we don't see, or maybe the hearts we're breaking without even knowing it." I catch Stan's eyes, and I let my gaze linger on him. "Everyone has a story. Maybe we should take the time to listen before it's too late."

The room is still. I can feel and hear the depth of each breath I take. I look over at Mary's neighbor, who is still hanging out in the aisle.

A signal. He needs a signal.

"Here's a fun fact," I continue in a slightly more upbeat tone. "Butterflies have an average life span of four weeks. A measly four weeks, most of which are spent inside a cocoon. When they emerge, they are these beautiful creatures that have no idea death is practically upon them. Fearless, beautiful creatures. Mary would have wanted us to be just that." I then end my speech with, "Let's be butterflies."

Well, that was not quite a poetic achievement, but the message was delivered. And so was the signal. Mary's neighbor releases what seems like hundreds of white butterflies. It is a sight to see.

After the soon-to-be-dead butterflies fled the scene, the feeling of sickness immediately came back tenfold. Silence takes over the room, above the noise of people quietly shuffling out the door. The still air is suffocating. I rush out of there as quickly as I can.

CHAPTER 14

Cory waits for me outside of the women's bathroom. I am greeted by a welcoming smile (or, maybe it is more like a smirk). He has a way of seamlessly interchanging the two. That little weasel. That loveable, empathetic weasel.

"'Let's be butterflies'?" he states with that half smile, half smirk of his. If it was anybody else, I would be embarrassed by what just transpired—the speech, the bolt to the ladies' room—but Cory has a way of making me feel normal in my flustered, less-than-flattering state. I need that kind of comfort right now and it comes in the form of Cory.

"Genius, right?" I say with the little sarcasm I'm able to muster.

"It was actually quite fitting. Mary would have loved it."

Cory and I catch a rideshare back to the office. I thought that Mary's neighbor was one of the most exuberant people I've ever encountered; that is, until I met our rideshare driver.

The ride back to the office was far from quiet. Our driver, whom I dubbed Daytime Santa based on his level of jolliness, spoke to us about the color spectrum. From the backseat, Cory and I received an unsolicited lesson about the optical spectrum, wavelengths, and frequencies. Of course, I can't retain this tidal wave of knowledge coming from Daytime Santa, but those are the highlights.

I don't judge; I simply listen. Cory and I glance at each other, and we immediately agree: Mary would have loved this.

We arrive at the office and bid adieu to our wonderful driver. I feel genuinely blessed to have met someone like *that* on a day like *this*. The Universe has a way of providing unexpected balance at times, doesn't it?

Cory and I get out of the car, and we watch Daytime Santa drive off. I turn to Cory and abruptly say, "Why don't you have a car? You can surely afford one."

"The environment, Sue," he responds with forced seriousness.

I scoff. I forget that he's from a batch of environmentally conscious youth. These self-aware, unentitled young people (yes, "unentitled" was not a typo). I'm skeptical yet pleased that they are trying to undo the destruction of past generations. Go on, you little rockstars.

It's funny, the places our mind goes during obscure situations. It's like a subconscious effort to avoid dwelling on one thing for too long. Perhaps it's part of our survival instincts. We want to avoid drowning in the depths of our emotions, particularly the sad ones. I thought about a lot today. The random, the weird, the happy—all of them ran through my mind like a marathon.

I am exhausted.

We enter the office. Barely a few feet in, and I see a stern-looking Michael rapidly approaching me. Here we go again. Bad juju incoming.

My new boss does not look happy. In fact, he hasn't been happy with me since I started on his team. He makes no effort to hide his disdain for my existence either. Luckily for him, I am too tired to care anymore. I remind myself that I'm only here for the paycheck. I do good work. I earned my promotion.

Michael hands me a pile of files (it was actually more like a toss). My arms are full. It took every ounce of me to not make a snarky comment about how he could have simply emailed me all of these documents. There is really no need to print out these files. But Michael needs the visual flairs—it's his style.

I know that Cory is counting the dead trees in his head as he stares at the stack of paper in my arms.

Cory and I just came from a funeral. *Mary's* funeral. This, whatever this is here with Michael, is not worth it (at least, not right now). We both refrain. We suppress the desire to punch Michael in his perfectly symmetrical face. Doing so would be very unprofessional. Visualizing it, however, is allowed. I'm seeing it happen multiple times in my head.

"I need this reviewed by the afternoon," Michael says gruffly. "If you were around this morning, you would have gotten more time." He turns around and proceeds to walk away.

He obviously disregarded the company memo about Mary's funeral this morning. This does not sit well with me. Not. One. Bit.

That's it! Why must I restrain myself around this kind of toxic person? Cory looks at me and senses the pent-up rage that's forthcoming. He takes a step back to allow me the space needed to unleash my fury. I will not allow Michael to put on this kind of display without any repercussions. He has gotten away with this kind of behavior too many times.

"Hey, Michael!" I yell at the back of his head, his perfectly groomed head of hair.

He turns around and stands there with an unamused look on his face. I hate his face so much right now. Never has such a pretty face simultaneously looks so punchable. His does.

Remember when I said that anger and sadness can provide you with unexpected confidence? Well, my friends, rage makes you *recklessly* bold. Rage is not what I want to fuel my fire, but alas, it ignites.

"At what point in your life did you decide you can get away with being an asshole?" I shout.

He offers no immediate response. He seems unaffected by my use of the word "asshole," as if he's been called that many times before.

He purposely walks slowly towards me. He does not give away much with his expression. When he gets close enough for me to read his face, I then recognize it immediately: unwavering cockiness.

Michael says, "Let me remind you that I am your boss—"

"Then act like one," I interrupt. He waits as if I'm going to continue, but there isn't much more to explain here. He's been acting like a little tyrant, and he knows it.

"Have those files reviewed by noon," Michael says, circling back to his demands.

I study his face. It, indeed, has gotten more punchable since the start of our interaction.

"No," I say calmly. I'm so done. If I can't put hands on him, I will find other ways to disrespect him. "What have *you* been doing all morning?" I press.

He wasn't expecting that judging by the way he repositioned his stance.

That's right. He better brace himself for Hurricane Sue.

"We went to pay our respects to our colleague," I continue. "In fact, most of the office were at the funeral. Actually, *all* of the managers were there, except one." I take a pause to let that sink in for him. "What were you doing this morning?" I ask again.

"Working," he quickly says. That cockiness is always right there beneath the surface, isn't it? It's never too far away to quickly reemerge at will. "You know, Sue, life does not stop for anybody. We continue on. We have things to do, deadlines to meet."

"Please don't try to give me a lesson on life right now." I put up my hand to stop him from saying any more. "I don't feel like taking any advice from a bullshitter. I can't do it today, Michael."

"I want those files reviewed by noon. Today," Michael says with a detectable aggravated tone. Did I make him crack a little? I hope so.

"No," I repeat as calmly as I can, although I can feel my knees shaking.

"Today, Sue," he reiterates as he takes a step closer to my face.

"No."

"Don't make me ask again." His eyes quickly change from annoyed to crazy in seconds. It's a little scary, I admit.

"No," I repeat. I don't know what came over me, but I smirked at him. I suppose I subconsciously wanted to mirror the asshole in front of me. "You are a piece of work," I continue, obviously omitting the word that I really wanted to use. I'm still very aware that I am at work and not out on the streets (as if Street Sue is that much different). No, Corporate Professional Sue is going to insult him as much as possible without getting fired.

"I am your boss," he says through tightened lips. "I will not tolerate this behavior."

"You are not my boss by choice."

We are both staring at each other intensely, as if our gaze could cause the other to spontaneously combust (a superpower that I truly wish I had, especially while in the presence of this villain).

"That's enough," says a loud stern voice out of the blue. Michael and I both turn towards the voice.

It's Cory, but a different version than his usual self.

Oh, shit.

CHAPTER 15

Did I cross the line? Was saying "no" to my boss too much for Cory to continue to stand by idly? I cannot believe that he is stopping me from unleashing my rage onto Michael. Cory, my support, my cheerleader. I thought he would root me on as I try to take down the white male patriarchy (in my own little way), but it seems that I misread my limits with him.

"Apologize," Cory says with an authoritative tone (which I didn't think was even possible).

I look at him incredulously. "Cory, I—"

"No, not you," Cory says. He looks directly at me as he pushes me aside and says, "Not everything is about you, you silly little bug." He then taps the top of my head. Wow. He really did that. On another day, at a different time, I will remind him that I am the older one in this odd friendship.

"Michael, apologize," Corey calmly says as he directs his attention to a very confused-looking Michael. Admittedly, I am too.

Michael scoffs. "Why are you always hanging around? Who are you?"

Apparently, word about Cory being the CEO's son *still* has yet to travel to Michael's ears. I'm not surprised, however. If it's not about Michael, it's not worth it for him to listen. Michael is the main character of his story and no one else, especially someone as unassuming as Cory, will ever take center stage.

"I'm Cory. Thank you for asking." Cory doesn't offer to elaborate on his job description (which I still don't know what that entails of either). He just leaves it at that and quickly gets back to his original point. "I just witnessed you pressure a colleague with unreasonable expectations. You need to apologize for your aggression."

Michael doesn't bother to respond to Cory. He looks so unamused by the entire situation. Maybe he is a little worn down by now. It's been a full fifteen minutes of this dreadful interaction. These are minutes we will never get back.

I'm running low on energy. I haven't eaten anything all morning. I just want this to end.

"Or we can get HR involved. Who doesn't love dealing with human resources?" Cory adds. "And, this wouldn't be the first time, right?"

"I suggest that you mind your own, *Cory.*"

Oh, the emphasis on his name! Are passive aggressive threats common amongst middle managers? It seems that way with Michael.

My stomach is growling. Hunger pains will soon follow. I can't do this anymore. I feel my body growing an ulcer as we stand here. I'm reminded why I don't like people in general. It physically hurts to be around some of them.

"I quit." They both immediately turn towards me.

Admittedly, those words escaped my mouth as if I'm just saying "hello" to another stranger in the halls. There was no oomph as one might expect. Those are some bold words to say out loud, yet my delivery lacked vigor.

"I don't need an apology from a piece of shit," I add. Alright, this second part may have made up for my previous lackluster statement. "Goodbye, *Michael*." Ha! I had to pull the same move; it felt right to emphasize his name the way one might scold a child.

So, that just happened. Street Sue made an appearance.

My dear readers, I may not love my job, but I do my job well. I would have retired (or died) here, whichever came first. The benefits are decent and, Hell, I just got a raise! I didn't plan on going anywhere. (I also have an aversion to job interviews, but that only played a minor-major role in my decision to stay put for so long). But, as they say, you don't leave a job, you leave the manager. It's true—it's so painfully true. My new boss, Michael, cannot compare—not even in the slightest way—to my old boss, Stan. To call them peers is unfair to Stan.

I hand over my stack of files to Cory.

If Michael is feeling any remorse for his actions, he's not showing it. Smugness sits on his face. I'm so sick of that face. It's obvious to me that the ugly in him has consumed his outer appearance. I can never unsee the ugly. I cringe at the thought that I ever admired this man.

As I'm walking towards the exit to my newly found freedom, I hear Cory speaking to Michael where I left them.

"It's going to be hard to fill her shoes," Cory casually says to Michael. "Looks like you're going to have to take on the extra work for a while. I would get to it."

He transfers the stack of paperwork into Michael's arms. I can hear Michael grumbling.

"Oh, and it needs to be reviewed by noon," Cory adds. I know that he purposely said it loud enough so that I could hear.

I'm beaming! This is what it feels like to have a personal cheerleader in life. My biggest fan is still at it. I know he's watching me with pride as I walk away from this situation.

A whole new world awaits just beyond these exit doors. It's pure adrenaline to walk away from the stable corporate life into the unknown, untamed world of unemployment. I can do anything! But first—I will delay conquering the world until after lunch. Priorities.

However, my plans for the rest of the afternoon—lunch and world domination—are quickly derailed. I step outside and I immediately see *him*.

My appetite is gone.

CHAPTER 16

He's wearing a suit. He usually doesn't wear a suit. I haven't seen him in a suit since that day he proposed and the day we decided to part. In case you need a refresher, both events happened on the same day—within minutes of each other. Paul, my would-have-been fiancé, is dressed in a navy suit with a white dress shirt and no tie. His hair is slicked back, and his face is perfectly framed by dark sunglasses.

I haven't missed Paul in *that* way. I miss my friend, sure, but I have forgotten those romantic feelings that once occupied my insides. I have yet to really dwell on the love lost. "Yet" being the key word here. I figure it will hit me eventually—out of nowhere as these feelings usually do—but it just has not. *Yet*.

As I watch him cross the busy intersection, I allow my eyes to look him up and down for longer than I should. He carries himself well—shoulders back, head high. The suit suits him.

There are no flutters here, only a longing for the comfort of an old friend. Do you ever hear a song and it immediately takes you back to a very specific time in your life? Paul is my song. I still remember all the lyrics.

I am staring hard now. Looking at him in this way could not possibly be good for my mental health, but I cannot take my eyes off him. Before I know it, he makes it over to my side of the street. He must have felt my stalkerish gaze. He takes off his sunglasses and begins walking in my direction.

I wonder if he'll walk right past me. If he does, perhaps he's still upset with me. But if he comes closer, does that mean he's over it? I don't know which one I prefer.

I will admit that for a split second—for a split of a split second—I wish I had said yes to his proposal. Here I am without a fiancé and now without a job. This is not exactly what I pictured for myself at this age. Paul is financially stable. I could have lived out my secret dream of being a stay-at-home wife. Surely, I will not have to worry about interviewing for a new job now that I am without one.

I momentarily curse my ambition to be a strong, independent woman. Damn my entire value system! I blame my mother.

"Hi, Sue."

…And I'm back. He apparently made his way to me as I entertained my silly little thoughts of being a pampered wife. Remember, that thought came to me at a moment of weakness. No judgment necessary.

Up close, I try to study his face for any indication of resentment. Does he still think about us and of what could have been? I ponder this while looking at his neat hair and clean-shaven face. But more importantly, the kindness in his eyes is still there. I am grateful for that.

He looks like he has his shit together. And truthfully, he always has. He was the same during our college days. While most of his friends got drunk and watched countless hours of anime on the weekend, Paul focused on his studies. He worked hard to graduate with honors, and he hasn't stopped working hard since. I'm proud of him. Of the two of us, he's much farther up the corporate ladder (as expected). I, on the other hand, am simply content whenever it's Free Lunch Fridays.

I feel my eyes start to well. Why? I don't know, but I wish for them to stop. From where he is standing, I imagine he's seeing a pitiful version of the girl he almost married. He must be thinking crisis avoided.

The welling turns into full-on tears. Once I start, it's hard to turn off the waterworks. I recognize that I am a mess.

Suddenly, I feel his arms around me. A rather unexpected move from my ex. His warm embrace helps calm my breathing. He lightens his hug, but I hold onto him. I want to stay in this moment for just a little longer. Paul, my friend, understands this. Without speaking, he holds my head against his chest and tells me that everything will be okay.

I smell the scent of his shirt. I know that he uses a particular detergent that is way too expensive for what it's worth. I know this because we have argued about said detergent. I would tell him that he keeps falling for the marketing of these overpriced detergents when the no-name brand is made up of the same ingredients (only with a much smaller marketing budget). He would tell me that it's okay to splurge on quality. And back and forth we go.

I spent the last few sentences telling you about detergent not to help you save a few bucks (although you will if you listen to me); I tell you this because smells can be powerful. Just like a song, it can evoke memories. There is comfort in the familiar. Paul's laundry detergent is familiar. The source of one of our many arguments—his overly marketed, overpriced detergent—smells like home.

This is dangerous.

How easily the past can draw you back in when the future is so uncertain. As I'm comforted by Paul's embrace, I know that I need to break away. If he holds me any longer, I may start planning our wedding. I'm vulnerable right now; it could happen.

All delusions aside, I know that this isn't right. I recognize the pull from the past and all of the romanticizing that is happening in my head. I stop it immediately. Songs and scents do not make the past relevant again. I will not recreate reality by reminiscing.

I take in one last whiff of his dress shirt, and I part, silently bidding adieu to the smell of an old love. I remind myself that we were better versions of ourselves when we were friends. I do hope that we can transition back to that. I don't have many friends to start with; I don't want to lose another.

Immediately after I deliver my unspoken eulogy for the death of this love affair, I hear, "Are you ready, Paul?"

This fresh-faced woman appeared out of nowhere. She must have descended from the clouds. She is dressed in form-fitting black slacks and a white button-up blouse. Her hair is perfectly pinned in an updo with a few strands loosely framing her delicate face. Absolutely stunning. Breathtaking in quite the literal sense. I momentarily forget to breathe at the sight of her natural beauty. I usually reserve such descriptions to describe mountains or other majestic scenery found in nature. Alas, I found a human form who can take on that honor.

Paul does not acknowledge her immediately (which is quite a feat if you're looking at what I'm looking at). Instead, he holds—or rather, squishes—my face in between the palm of his hands and asks, "Are you good?"

I break my gaze away from Ms. Blessed Genes and bring my attention back to Paul. I nod. "All good here." Hardly believable, I know.

Paul then introduces me to Ms. Blessed Genes and then he turns to me. "This is my...," he gestures in my direction and pauses, "friend." Oh, the pause says a lot! It did not go unnoticed.

I'm content with "friend" (I think).

Paul goes on to let me know that they are cutting out of work early to get a jump start on the weekend. The two of them. Just the two of them. He didn't exactly stress that last part in particular, but as I watched Ms. Blessed Genes loop her arms around his, I got the message loud and clear.

We say our goodbyes.

Well, that hurt more than I expected. I can't remember a time when Paul ever stopped working early to go have some fun. Not on my birthday. Not on the day he proposed. Not even on the day I got food poisoning (albeit he was the one who warned me to not frequent a particular beloved taco truck so much). Nonetheless, Paul leaving work early was never a thing during our relationship. Ever. Never.

Interesting. Or rather, what the hell?

I need to keep it together. I'm more bothered by this revelation than I should be. I'm sure they are still looking at me as I'm walking away. I feel the weight of their pity-stares. I should not turn around and torment myself with one last glimpse of the two of them, as a couple, perfectly fitting with one another. *Keep it together, girl. Keep walking.*

I need to get to my safe space. *But where the fuck is that?*

Today is the day of ending things, it seems. The funeral, my job, this relationship—all done and gone. What other things can I put an end to today?

Let's start with my hunger. I haven't eaten all morning.

As if the Gods were listening to my internal turmoil, my safe space appeared right in front of me after all of my aimless walking. There it is: a coffee shop located right next to a dive bar.

Fuck songs and scents. There will be no crying when I'm stuffing my face.

CHAPTER 17

I wake up and I feel the weight of his arms around me. We fell asleep in this awkward cuddle position and to my dismay, he didn't move all night—and neither did I.

I do a ninja-esque move to carefully untangle myself from his warm body without waking him. I succeed in my maneuver.

With our bodies now inches apart, I lay there facing him as still as I possibly can. I know that I have only a short window before this peace and quiet ends. And so, I savor it while it lasts.

He looks content asleep. The usual stress and worries that plague him during the day are not present on his face as he lays here. It's strange—I've looked at this man so many times in my life, but now that he is in my room, on my bed, in my sheets, his face takes on a different light.

His dark eyelashes rest against his tan skin. I watch and wait to see if his closed eyes flutter in his sleep. They don't. I think about those eyes, those gentle brown eyes that stared so deeply into mine last night. Yes, those same eyes that led us to where we are now: in my bed, in my tiny apartment.

I study the shape of his lips—his lovely full lips—and I feel compelled to reach out and touch them. I don't for fear of waking him.

I feel flushed.

Naturally, I let my eyes wander farther down to his neck and then onto his bare shoulders. It's not hard to notice the definition in his arms as he hugs the sheets in the absence of my body. I find myself wanting to be enveloped in those arms again. But I refrain and instead, I watch his sculpted chest move up and down as he breathes lightly in and out. The rhythmic pattern of his breathing is occasionally interrupted by what I imagine are dreams dancing around his head.

I want to know what his dreams are about.

This man has been in my blind spot for so long and now that he is clearly within view, I cannot take my eyes off him. I am at ease with what I see in front of me. I have managed to resist his gravitational pull for some time, but he now has me within his orbit, and I would like to stay here.

He slowly opens his eyes. When those deep brown eyes find mine, he smiles. It's the kind of smile that dances in the corner of the eyes; a smile so honest, it's endearing.

Dare I say, he looks happy? I'll say it. He looks happy.

Am I?

I know, I skipped quite a few details here. My dear readers, you are probably confused at this point. That's understandable and perhaps even an understatement. Before I divulge the name of the man lying beside me right now, allow me to live in this moment a little longer.

Things are calm and comfortable. I want to hold onto this because it's about to get complicated.

CHAPTER 18

The sun is shining through my apartment window with intensity this morning. The sunlight is usually welcomed, but right now it's keeping me from getting extra sleep. I continue to lay here in my bed and force my eyelids to remain closed. It's not working though. My body wants to sleep, but my mind has a different agenda. Thoughts of all things thinkable flood in at once. I wish I could just turn it off at will—the sunshine and my mind.

It's Monday, and I have nowhere to be.

I have no urgent emails to address, no phone calls to make, no deadlines to meet. I am jobless, and I have absolutely no plans for the day ahead.

Am I living the dream?

It's a blessing and a curse, I suppose. I now have the gift of time. I can choose to sleep for hours on end (after investing in some blackout curtains) or learn a new skill (competitive eating currently tops the list). The options are endless now without a job commitment to tie me down. However, rent will be due soon, as it is every damn month. I have student loans to pay. The same loans that allowed me to go to college in order to secure the job that I just quit (funny how that played out). And I have utility bills due because, you know, the whole "living" thing.

Human life can be overly complicated.

My thoughts wander back to my old job, my beloved cubicle, the free coffee. I replay my big "I Quit!" moment over and over again. The triumph I felt as I marched out of the office that day is, well, less triumphant now. I gave up my only source of income as I walked out on my toxic boss. Bold or stupid? It's rhetorical; no need to answer that.

Almost ninety-nine percent of the things we regret saying could have been avoided if we just waited it out. If we had just stopped—if we had just let our emotions settle first—certain words would not have escaped our heated heads, where (let's be honest) most things should stay forever put.

In my case, had I just waited for the immediate anger to subside, and had I eaten something prior to my run-in with Michael, I may not have quit my comfortable, cushy job. With a clear head (and a full tummy), I would have seen the situation for what it was: a lose-lose one for me. If I stayed on the team, I would feel Michael's wrath daily because he obviously despises me. If I leave, well, there goes my livelihood. Regardless, had I not quit on the spot, I would not be worried about my cashflow right now. And that flow is a-drying, especially considering how much money I spent on take-out this past weekend in order to make myself feel better. The "I deserve this" mantra can really hurt the wallet sometimes.

Then, thoughts of the past weekend reentered my mind in a flash—with fervor. Thoughts of work are quickly replaced with thoughts of *him*. It wasn't long ago that he kept this bed warm. I replay our gentle entanglements and relive every touch. I'm smiling without realizing I'm doing so; I know this only because my face starts to hurt. I momentarily forget about the job that I don't have. *Very* momentarily.

The sunshine is relentless. It's now burning my eyelids. My eyeballs are up next to feel the sun's wrath.

I finally sit up. I call this progress. *Now what?*

I decide it's too soon—too raw—to fix the work situation. I will stay in my pajamas today and binge watch *The Last Kingdom*. (It's an amazing show for those of you who have not yet blessed your eyeballs with this gem of a television series. And for those of you who know exactly what I'm talking about, you are my people).

Before I could get to my tv-watching marathon, there's a soft knock at my door. I look down and do a quick check of myself. I'm dressed *enough*. My pajamas are covered with images of dogs wearing sunglasses; it'll have to do.

I go to the door. Surprisingly (but not so surprisingly), it's Cory. I told you before, he has a knack for invading my personal space. It's now his signature move.

He comes with iced coffee in hand. I forgive him for the intrusion immediately.

"I thought I should do a wellness check considering…you know," Cory says as he steps into my tiny apartment without waiting for an invite to come inside.

I allow it.

"I'm good. I'm good," I say about a few times too many and too quickly.

He takes a quick look around my place. A *very* quick look. I imagine my apartment is the size of a modest shoe box compared to what he's accustomed to. All he needs to do is stand in one spot and make a full circle. Home tour complete.

"Now that I've confirmed you are alive and well…enough," he says as he checks out my choice of sleepwear, "I wanted to remind you that the annual charity event is this Saturday."

"I can't go. I'm no longer an employee, remember?" I say.

"Be my plus one."

I take a moment. He sees my hesitation.

"Why not?" he asks. "We don't need to split the rideshare; I'll pay for the entire thing."

I smile. Either he wants to make me laugh or he's frugal. Either way, it amuses me.

"We can both avoid Michael together," he says.

"Why do *you* need to avoid *him?*"

"He found out about my connection to the CEO aka 'Mommy.' Now he wants to be besties."

I nod. That sounds like Michael, always working an angle.

"Careful. He's ambitious. He might try to become your stepdad."

Cory snorts. I love it. Snorts get a bad rep, but it's truly a wonderful sound that comes from a place of happiness. We should all snort more often.

I down my iced coffee in a few gulps.

Cory, per usual, makes me forget about my immediate worries. The iced coffee helps too.

He smiles at me. His boyish smile overflows with authenticity; it's the kind that reminds me of rainbows and unicorns.

Suddenly, thoughts of Mary rush into my mind. Just like that. I don't know how I jumped from snorts to sadness. It hasn't been too long since her funeral and admittedly, I have not felt this kind of emptiness since. I miss her presence. I miss *her*. It's strange how the mind works. Like I said, if only I could turn my mind off at will. There should be an app for that. Someday, I'm sure there will be.

I lose myself in thought and my smile no longer holds its form.

Without hesitation and not a moment wasted, Cory steps in closer and gives me a hug with his entire body. I can feel my organs squish against each other as Cory squeezes his arms around me. It's that kind of hug. It's like he wants to intentionally overwhelm me with his embrace to stifle my own overwhelming feelings. It's brilliantly emphatic and affectionate. And very effective.

I snap out of it.

How did this beautiful being enter my inner circle so quickly? Very few have managed to do so in all my years of actively shunning people. We went from strangers to—dare I say—friends so naturally. It's quite an achievement considering how good I am at repelling people. I ought to get certified for such a skill. I am talking about years and years (and years and years) of skepticism and mistrust of others compounding over time. It is an Olympic feat to break through my walls. Well done, Cory.

I find most people exhausting. He, on the other hand, radiates.

He lightens up his hug (thankfully). I can breathe again. As he moves away, I can see that his eyes are fixated on something. I follow his line of sight towards the object of his attention.

"Who's baseball cap is that?" he asks with his classic half smirk, half smile.

I stare at the faded Oakland baseball cap resting on my nightstand. I don't answer.

We both know he knows the answer to his own question.

CHAPTER 19

I have to admit, I'm looking fairly decent tonight. I put in the extra effort to run a comb through my hair and managed to squeeze myself into a dress that is half a size too small. Not bad.

Saturday night is already here. I spent the majority of this week worrying about the charity ball. And now, I am standing outside on the steps of the event hall. I am surprised that I even made it this far.

On my arm is a rather dapper-looking Cory. Is he on my arm or am I on his? It's hard to tell. We are both linked at the elbows, and I don't plan on unlinking for the rest of the night. I need him to hold me up—literally. These heels are impossible to walk in.

Cory wears a classic black suit with no tie. His hair is combed back with just enough gel to still be a little unruly. That boyish charm is hard to smother. It works for him.

I lead Cory up the stairs. There's no point in letting the social anxiety build up while we stand outside in the cold. We are here now. We should go and be anxious inside where it's a little warmer at least. More importantly, food awaits just beyond these doors.

"Let's go be weird," he says.

I smile. My sentiments, exactly.

Not more than fifteen minutes upon entering the grand ballroom, a flood of people start making their way to us. Well, not exactly to *us*. They are obviously making a beeline to Cory. My plan of not unlinking arms with him is quickly thwarted by the swarm of people waiting to make small talk with the CEO's son.

This is my worst nightmare. People. Lots of them.

I let go of Cory. He shoots me a look that tells me he understands my need to flee.

"I'll find you," he says before bracing himself for the inevitable shallow conversations that await.

I escape before anyone could offer me their obligatory greetings. Do we shake hands? Do we hug? Do we simply nod and force a smile, the kind where the eyes are a little too strained? It's hard for me to figure out the right play for these micro interactions. And so, I avoid them. At this point, my aversion to social encounters should not surprise you.

I walk on, staying close to the walls. This isn't because I'm a wallflower. Just because I don't like talking to people don't mean I don't like to dance. I'm preemptively relying on these sturdy walls to hold me up for when I trip over my own gown. This isn't my first rodeo; I know that a clumsy fall is in my future tonight. (And yet, I haven't learned that pant suits are the way to go. Next year, perhaps).

I happily take a drink from one of the servers carrying a plethora of liquid refreshments. I don't know what exactly is in this glass, but the server made sure to let me know that it was not a virgin. That'll do.

The ballroom is decorated exquisitely with oversized chandeliers and garlands of white flowers and gold ribbons. The gold ribbon is the awareness symbol for childhood cancer. This is the main reason I'm here. It's the reason why I plant myself into these social situations. I *can't* miss this event, and I haven't missed one in all the years I've been with the company.

Every year, the company chooses a different charity related to children's cancer. It's a lavish event attached to a sad cause. Perhaps the elaborate and excessive decor distracts us from talking about children dying. It's a downer of a subject, of course. We are here for the kids, but we also want to enjoy the night. That's the uncomfortable truth.

I finish my cursory scan of the ballroom. No immediate threats found. I walk on and then I hear boisterous laughter from a small group of people huddled together in the center of the room. The laughter all subsides at the same time.

Whenever I hear synchronous laughing, I immediately think that it's all a little contrived. Such animated laughter, the kind that ends with complete silence or collective sighs, is usually reserved for someone who needs to be impressed or appeased or, I don't know, loved? Why else would we fake a laugh? It depends on who it's for.

In this case, the collective laughter is for Michael, my latest ex-boss. *Now* that laughter makes sense. Michael needs an audience; it gives him some kind of affirmation of his importance.

I watch him do his crowd work from afar. It is a talent to have the energy for all of that. However, I can see the sadness sneak upon his face as soon as the talk dies down and the smile disappears. His resting look is somber, even if it's just for a second. It's clear from where I'm standing. By being outside of the commotion, I'm able to see it clearly—the stiff smiles and all that social fluff that takes up too much airspace.

He's troubled.

It's in this moment that he spots me from where he stands and begins to make his way over. I study his face as he approaches. The old me would have screamed inside to see such an alluring, captivating face walking my way. Clearly, he's not the same person in my eyes as he was before. Hell, he's not the same person he was just moments earlier when surrounded by an audience. After all that we've been through, I no longer feel the nerves, the intimidation, the insecurities. All of that is gone.

I am so fixated on Michael that I am startled by a hand on my shoulder. I turn around. It's Stan. He's dressed in a dark charcoal suit and gold tie (to tie into tonight's cause). It makes me happy to see him sporting gold. The reason for tonight's social affair is not lost on some.

Before I could offer my greetings, I hear, "Can I talk to you, Sue?" It's both Stan and Michael, almost simultaneously. I don't know who I should acknowledge first.

Do you remember when I said that things were about to get complicated (after my whirlwind weekend with the-man-I-will-not-name)?

It's about that time.

I'm standing between two men who outwardly can't stand one another, and whose personalities are on the opposite ends of the spectrum. These are the same two men who have caused me to swing back and forth on a pendulum of emotions like the unstable adult that I am.

Well, one of them, I allowed into my bed.

Hello, Complication.

CHAPTER 20

Michael looks at me with pleading eyes. He is, again, using his best asset: his face. He's fully aware that he is good-looking and he's surely putting those chiseled features to use. If you couple his face with sad eyes, well, it just isn't fair. I don't stand a chance of refusing his request to speak privately. So, I will acquiesce, but with necessary caution.

The situation, as it is, is a delicate one.

I give Stan my most sympathetic smile, and I tell him I will be right back. He returns my smile with his own, and quite frankly, his smile gave me a boost of confidence that I was not expecting. It was a subtle affirmation that he will patiently wait his turn, and it made me feel empowered.

I know that Stan is watching me as I walk away with Michael by my side. It makes me self-conscious (more so than I already am). I do my best to look competent in these heels. The struggle is real, however.

It's amazing how my choice of footwear can impact the entire night. I've never related to Cinderella more in my entire life than I do now. However, she nabbed a prince. It's too early to tell what my fancy footwear will do for me tonight. Let's hope it doesn't involve any running.

I digress, as is often the case when I'm trying to think of anything other than what's currently occupying my headspace. And that is, the very real danger of falling flat on my face. The probability is high.

I unwillingly use Michael's arm for additional support. He doesn't seem to mind. In fact, he shortens his stride and slows down his pace. I appreciate the courtesy, but I loathe that he can tell I'm struggling.

As soon as we reach a quiet corner of the ballroom, Michael faces me with his entire body. Instead of meeting my eyes, however, he stares at the floor. This is strange. His usual outwardly loud confidence is replaced with that of a sheep. It's unsettling for a man like him. But, like I mentioned before, the situation is delicate; perhaps he's trying to figure out how to navigate the new tide.

As am I.

Michael finally looks at me in the eyes and says slowly, "I am so sorry. I messed up."

I feel the sincerity in his words immediately. Or, more accurately, I feel it in the way he looked at me. I may be a fool for taking his words at face value, but *his* face—his blatantly handsome face—is working overtime to make me believe his words. Pretty privilege is real.

I, of course, will not let him in on my thoughts. I decide it's best to not offer a verbal response. This isn't a devised power play; I'm still processing everything that's happened between us. And everything is a lot.

Michael continues, "I think about you often lately, and every time, I imagine a scenario in which you forgive me. Sue, please forgive me."

His eyes do not stop working their magical powers in between his sentences. Let me tell you, it takes Herculean-level effort to not be drawn in. But I cannot—I will not—succumb to his superficial magnetism, which is surprisingly still…magnetic. (I know, I'm quite the wordsmith).

And so, I remain silent.

In the absence of a response from me, he inches his body closer to mine. We are only a breath away from each other. The silence fills the space between us. My discomfort level starts to rise.

"The truth is," Michael says as he stares at my mouth, "I've been wanting to…" He suddenly tries to meet his lips with mine.

I push him away immediately. This must be a joke that no one gets. The sincerity that I thought was in his apology was all in my head. This is in no way sincere. My gut tells me this is calculated (and cunning). I kick myself for letting him get this close and for entertaining his attempt to display actual human emotions. It's pitiful.

"What is this?" I ask as I give him a look of disgust. He shrinks back, surprised by my reaction. I'm surprised that he's surprised, as if he thought I would just let this atrocious moment play out the way he envisioned. The size of his ego is nauseating.

When I didn't immediately gush over his apology, did he feel the need to take it a step farther? I am unmoved and appalled by his contrived confession of any romantic feelings towards me. Moments like these cannot be orchestrated with a covert agenda and without sincerity.

"What do you want from me?" Michael asks. The softness in his voice from before is gone.

"Nothing. There's nothing you can offer me."

"I'm trying my best here, Sue."

"Your best is to try to seduce me? Do you need to exert some kind of power over me? Is this your way to earn forgiveness?" I ask rhetorically.

The sadness in his eyes is still there. I know, however, that it's not due to some unrequited love or any longingness for me. I am not the object of his affection. Whatever is troubling him is beyond what I can help him with.

"I *am* sorry, Sue."

His eyes, with their unrelenting ability to draw you in, cannot hide his sorrow. I realize now that I had mistaken his sadness for sincerity.

"Who hurt you, Michael?" I ask calmly without fully wanting to know the answer. There is too much to unpack with that question. He knows it too. He hesitates to respond.

"Forgive me, Sue," he finally says.

I take one last look at his face as I try to search for some semblance of authenticity; I find only sadness. But surprisingly,

I do forgive him. He's obviously fighting other demons. His issue is bigger than me.

Still, I do not communicate what I'm thinking. I do not offer him any comfort; I do not owe him anything. I don't intend to fix something I didn't break.

I turn my back to him and walk away. I do not wish to ever revisit this mess.

I need some air.

I scan the room for the nearest exit and head towards it. I manage to walk a distance without once thinking about how these damn heels could end me. That is, until I finally exit the ballroom and the cold air outside brings back all thoughts of how uncomfortable I am—physically and emotionally.

I take a seat on the steps of the grand entrance (or more like the grand exit in my case). I immediately take off my heels to relieve my soles. The cold hard surface of the cement feels good beneath my feet. There is something cathartic about wearing a formal gown in bare feet.

It's cold, but I welcome the breeze. I close my eyes and allow the fresh air to cool my heated head.

Michael. He is something, isn't he? I chuckle as I think back to the time when his presence would make me forget most of my vocabulary. I admired him (never in a romantic kind of way); I viewed him as a unicorn amongst us. And now, I feel nothing. After all that we've been through, I feel nothing when I look at him. And I prefer it that way.

At this point in my story, I think you figured out that it wasn't Michael who slept in my bed. I could never allow such a man to get that close to me. I need to keep my home a safe space, and Michael gives me no feelings of security nor comfort. Like I mentioned, I feel nothing.

I stare at my feet which are still planted firmly on the steps of the Grand Hall. I painted my nails gold for tonight's occasion. They are gold, with more gold sparkles on top. It's a detail that most people would gloss over, but I thought it mattered tonight.

And I was right.

As I sit on these steps and stare at my painted toenails, I'm reminded of why I made the effort to be here in the first place: childhood cancer. *What the hell do I have to sulk about?*

It's time to get off these steps, put on my big-girl heels, and do some lightweight drunk-dancing all in the name of a good cause.

But just as I am about to get up off my bum, I feel someone take a seat right next to me. I don't see the person first; I see their toes.

She has also taken off her heels and is letting her feet breathe. Her toes are painted gold.

I smile from ear to ear. Details do matter.

"Are we kindred spirits?" she asks whimsically. She must have noticed the detail too.

I look up from her toes to meet her eyes. Holy Guacamole! It's Angela Lee. It's the CEO. It's Cory's mom. I registered all those things in that very order.

"If kindred spirits mean I will be as successful as you, then I sure hope so," I say. "And by successful, I do mean wealthy, preferably filthy rich."

She laughs with her entire being. It is a laughter that I can appreciate.

"You're Sue," she says.

"You're Angela Lee."

"Cory talks about you. *A lot*. He pointed you out to me back there." She gestures towards the ballroom. "I would like to ask you to 'unquit.' I have a new role for you. And don't worry, you will not report into Michael."

Well, that took an unexpected turn—and rather quickly. She wastes no time.

"I didn't get where I am without having some guts," she says as she smiles at me, "and some help."

"Did Cory ask you to help me?" I ask.

"Of course, he did."

"Of course, he did," I repeat more to myself than to her.

"To be wealthy—or filthy rich, in your case—it helps to start with a job," Angela says.

"Strange concept," I reply.

She chuckles. She gets up from the steps and reaches out her hand. I take it and hoist myself onto my feet.

"Let's go dance. There are kids dying every day. The least we can do is dance," Angela says. "Let's see if we can find Michael on the dance floor and accidentally kick him." She winks at me.

"I'll gladly follow your lead."

I can see why Cory turned out the way he did. He's lucky to have this strong woman in his life. Strangely, my thinking about him must have summoned him. Out of nowhere, Cory links his arm with mine, and wraps his other arm around his mother's shoulder. The three of us walk back towards the party together.

"So, are you coming back to work on Monday?" Cory asks me in a whisper.

"Let's get through this night first."

CHAPTER 21

Here I am again, walking into my office building, my begrudged second home for the past six years. It's only been a week since my dramatic resignation, yet it already feels different to be within these walls again.

It's unsettling (and sad) how the familiar can change so quickly.

It's early. I made sure to get here before everyone else starts to file in. It's quiet at this hour. It's eerie to see this place void of people when it's normally a cesspool of germs, but it's strangely peaceful now. The emptiness provides calmness, which is exactly what I need today.

I walk the halls alone.

When I pass the beloved breakroom, I immediately miss Mary. I miss the coffee she makes every morning. There is no one as enthusiastic as her when it came to making coffee. Not even a close second. *God, I miss her.* I wonder who took over coffee duty since her passing. Regardless, the coffee will never taste the same.

I continue on my way to my cubicle, which has been abandoned for all of an entire week. The dust bunnies must be running amok.

I walk past the usual row of manager offices, and then I hear, "Sue, please come in."

The hairs on the back of my neck stand up. I was not expecting anyone to be here this early in the morning.

The door to Stan's office is open. It's only 7:15 AM. I should have known that he, of all people, would be the one to show up early, especially on a day when I planned to be inconspicuous.

He swiftly gets up from his desk and meets me in the doorway.

"Hi," I say in my most pretend-this-isn't-awkward tone. I haven't talked to him since the charity event and by "talk" I mean by saying "I'll be right back" and then never doing so.

"I heard Angela Lee offered you the consultant role," he says with a smile that is as genuine as a posed social media photo. Something is bothering him. I've studied his face long enough to know the difference between his real smile (which is a rare sighting up until recently) and his forced smile. This one is forced; sadness is weighing down at its corners.

"She did offer me that role," I say. I feel my face mirroring his; my smile makes an obligatory appearance, but my eyes do not match it. The space between us has a subtle air of despair—subtle, but enough to recognize it.

"I hope this does not change anything between us," he says.

"What exactly is between us?" I challenge. I've been wanting to know the answer to that question. We have not spoken more than a few words to each other since we spent that night together in my small apartment.

In case you haven't figured it out by now, the person who slept beside me was no other than Stan. Yes, *this* Stan, my former boss, the same man who's standing in front of me now. I must stress the "slept beside me" part. We cuddled in bed and fell asleep with his arms wrapped around me. In a lot of ways, I could argue that it was more intimate than sex, and a hell of a lot more confusing.

That night, he showed up at my door after he heard the news that I walked out on Michael (remember, we quit the boss, not the job). Stan wanted to come by to say goodbye, but it seemed that by the end of the night, we started a new chapter instead.

Allow me to explain.

* * *

I was feeling low having just quit my job and then running into my ex-almost-fiancé, Paul, with his abnormally beautiful new girlfriend. Moreover, this was all after attending Mary's funeral just earlier in the day (because the Universe decided I needed to be kicked while I'm down). Well, the Universe delivered. I was down—*really* down—and far from my usual delightful self (shocker!). And then, Stan, with whom I have a very confusing relationship, shows up at my apartment door to add to my emotional whirlwind.

Stan told me that he was saddened by the news of my departure. It would be a major adjustment for him to no longer see me every day in the office. He wanted to let me know that he would miss me, and he needed to let me know this in person before he lost the courage to do so.

Now, at this point, I soak this all up because I needed *something,* and the Universe decided to send me Stan as a pick-me-up after knocking me down. *You're not forgiven, Universe, but I will go with it.* I liked what I was hearing from Stan. I threw my arms around his neck and pulled him in. I needed this. I think he sensed it too. His embrace was a welcomed interruption to my pity party.

I remember feeling so low that my only other option was to laugh (in order to balance the emotional scale). And so, I laughed through my tears. Stan was there the entire night to laugh with me. We also talked—a lot. We talked like old buddies catching up with one another. Perhaps the setting of my tiny apartment facilitated this kind of banter; it never happened at the office before.

My tiny apartment also facilitated Stan to lay down on my bed. To be fair, there was no other space for him to stretch out. I joined him because it is *my* bed, after all, and it is the most comfortable place in my apartment.

When the laughing died down and our eyes grew heavier, he asked if I wanted him to leave. I chose to close the distance between us even more and buried myself in his arms. And there, he stayed until the morning.

It was a kind, gentle moment that will forever live in my head. But the moment was also clouded with confusion as it ignited all sorts of feelings I never thought I harbored for Stan. All of that talking, and laughing, and intimacy, yet we never talked about *us*. I knew, however, where I stood after that night. I wanted him. Only him.

* * *

Now that Stan is in front of me and we are again alone together, my unsettled feelings are bubbling to the surface.

It's time to unpack this relationship.

"I don't know what is between us," I say to Stan. I can see his eyes shift nervously. "If you don't want anything to change between us, then we won't be more than what we are."

"That's not what I want, Sue," he says.

"So, what do you want?" My tone is reluctantly pleading. I know what I need to hear, and who I want to hear it from. I need to hear it directly and clearly. "Are you happy I was offered this new role? Then we can go back to our professional working relationship."

The sadness behind his eyes is now center stage. His forced smile can no longer hold its form.

"How can you say that, Sue?" he asks. "I cannot go back to the way things were. I've waited for you for so long."

I say nothing. I need to hear more.

I can see he's struggling to find the right words as he places his hands into his pockets and lets his eyes fall to his feet. When I see a grown man display such boyish mannerisms, I know that he is hurting or is too afraid to reveal the truth. Maybe both.

When he finally looks up and meets my eyes, I feel a nervousness that I cannot control. I'm not visibly shaking, but I might as well be. The floor beneath me feels unstable although I'm standing still. I have never—in my thirty-something years of living—had a man look at me so wistfully. I see the vulnerability in his eyes and like contagion, it also makes me weak.

"Sue," he says softly, "I tried my best to not let you get to me. But you got to me long ago and I'm still unable to shake your grasp, maybe more so now than before."

He retreats his footsteps and leans against his desk for support. He lowers his head as if he just realized the weight of his words.

I'm grateful for the momentary break from his stare; it gives me a moment to remember to breathe.

"I've tried so hard to not look at you a certain way," Stan continues as his eyes find mine again. "You became all that I could think about. But by the time I recognized these feelings for what they were—still are—you were already in a relationship. And then you got engaged, or at least I thought you were, and I didn't know what to do. I still don't. I'm afraid to mess this up."

He pushes himself off his desk and moves toward me. The longingness in his eyes holds me hostage. I cannot move. I've even forgotten how to blink since he started talking. My systems are shutting down—all essential functions have disabled.

I may need a minute to brace myself. This is a lot coming from a man who has been my boss for so many years. This is also the same man who I have not been able to stop thinking about. It's jarring that he's the same person. I need to reset.

"I'm yours, Sue. I've always been yours."

There. As clear as day. I can never unhear those words. We can never go back to the way things were.

My eyes dart to the clock on the wall behind him. It is 7:40 AM.

"I need to go," I say as if this is just another casual conversation that I needed to end.

If he held his breath this entire time, he finally exhaled. His shoulders give way to the weight of my indifference.

I cannot bear to see him this way. I immediately reach out to touch his arm, and then I gently place a kiss on his cheek. He lets out a sigh of relief at my attempt to reassure him.

"I will be right back," I say. "I mean it this time." That made him smile. I love that smile. It's the same one he wore when he woke up next to me for the first time. I can never forget it.

He rubs his palm on the back of his neck. He looks away but not before I catch him biting his bottom lip as if to contain his excitement. It's simply endearing.

"Congrats on the new job, Sue," he says. Then he quickly adds, "I will quit mine if there's a conflict of interest."

That smile, on *that* face, can revive a heartbeat. It took all of me to refrain from throwing myself at him. I need to break away from his pull while I still have the willpower to do so.

"There's something I need to do. I will be right back," I say, reassuring him again.

As soon as I walk out of his view, my eyes begin to well. I've never before been moved to the point of happy tears. This feeling is new. This is the first time I've ever felt wanted, acknowledged, loved. It is overwhelming in the most welcoming way. If this is what it feels to love and be loved, then I don't think I've ever loved before him.

CHAPTER 22

As agreed upon, Cory meets me at my desk at exactly 7:45 AM. It then takes me all of a whole minute to clear out my things.

I turned down Angela's Lee job offer on the night of the charity ball. It was too soon to unquit. As much as she emphasized that I will not have to work with Michael anymore, I recognize that a person's toxicity is permeable. It will find a way to get to me. The three and a half walls of my cubicle are not strong enough to keep it out. I needed a change and, perhaps, Michael was the needed push for me to make one (as ugly as that all went down).

When I told Cory that I would not take the job, he wanted to be there while I gather my belongings and bid my silent goodbyes to inanimate objects and the familiar spaces around the office. I told him my plan, and he decided that he wanted to witness my sentimental weirdness in person.

Today's that day.

Goodbye photocopier that always jammed when it was my turn. Goodbye my beloved stapler (I love the sound a good stapler makes). Goodbye women's bathroom, my haven from obligatory office socializing. I will especially miss this hallway, the one that leads me straight to the exit of the end of each day.

I feel Cory's eyes on me as I walk around, slowly touching things that probably no one has really touched before (I'm talking about the walls, the whiteboards in the meeting rooms, the fire extinguisher). If he thinks I'm being weird, he is certainly letting me indulge as he patiently watches me.

"Are you almost done?" Cory asks as we walk past a row of closed office doors.

"Nope." I respond with excitement. I'm practically skipping down this hallway.

"Okay, just checking. But you do know that it's close to eight, which means people will start to file in, which means there will be questions asked."

I stop whatever I was doing, which is, in the moment, saying goodbye to the coffee pot. He's right. I need to get out of here before the awkward goodbyes ensue.

We head towards the exit. Usually, this route would make me giddy at the end of each day, but that feeling is now replaced with a sentimental sadness. I don't dwell on the feeling too long, however. There is one last thing I need to do before I officially remove myself from this building.

I stop Cory from marching forward as we arrive just outside of Stan's office. I peek inside and I see Stan behind his desk, staring off into his computer screen. He sees me enter and immediately gets up.

"Dinner tonight? Korean?" I ask him. "Also, I no longer work here."

He smiles, albeit a bit confused.

"I need an answer before security escorts me out," I say as I nudge towards Cory who's right outside of the doorway.

"I'll pick you up at six," he replies. He then looks at Cory, who just happens to be staring back at that very moment. "Will he be joining us?"

"I'm sure he would love to, but that's a hard no. We—you and I—are going on a date. You've made me wait long enough."

Stan rushes over and wraps his arms around me. I disappear within his embrace. I catch the scent of his clothes. It smells like fresh clean laundry without the extra perfume. I take it in as I think of the memories this scent will one day evoke. I love that this scent is his.

"We need to go," Cory says.

His voice snaps me out of my laundry aromatherapy thoughts. He is, again, right. We need to make a quick exit.

Once outside the building, I take one last look at the exterior of the office. This place once filled me with dread every workday morning. That feeling is now gone as I stare at the building's hideous facade. What I used to dread is now what I will miss. I will miss this ugly building.

Cory sees that I'm in my feelings (I think that's how the younger kids these days describe "being emotional"). He says, "You *do* remember that you are going to meet me here for lunch tomorrow, right?"

I'm quickly reminded that I will be back. But it won't be the same, will it? I will no longer come here to earn a paycheck; I will actually come here by choice—by my own freewill!

Again, I must repeat how quickly the familiar becomes strange. And, by the same token, how quickly the strange becomes, well, no longer that. Case in point: the person by my side now who is waiting patiently for me to say my final goodbye to this horrendous-looking office building.

This workplace has given me a lot. Work experience, sure, but this place also gave me Cory. He has no idea (or perhaps he does) how quickly he became a friend for when I needed one, for when I didn't know I needed one, at the one place I never intended to make friends to begin with.

Am I evolving as a person? This must be what progress feels like. Strange.

I suppose we all need a catalyst for change. Mine wasn't anything too dramatic, but it was the most impactful in the simplest form. Mine was a once-stranger named Cory. This is only the start of how much he will change my life.

Hello, New Beginnings.

CHAPTER 23

I sit back and watch the bride and groom perform their first dance. The song selection is amazing. It's a Bruno Mars song (not one of his singles that got an excessive amount of airplay); this one is called "The Rest of My Life" and it's devastatingly beautiful.

I don't feel any regret as I watch my ex-boyfriend-almost-fiancé, Paul, dance with his new wife, whose beauty is even more amplified in a form-fitting white wedding gown (again, the looks game can be so unfair). If I regret anything right now, it's my years of poor diet and lack of exercise.

I digress, as is often the case when my eyeballs are staring at someone this beautiful, almost as beautiful as the Bruno Mars' song playing overhead. Both of which can bring me to tears.

Like I said, no regrets. Paul seems happy. His toothy smile says a lot, but it's in the way he looks at her, and even more importantly, how she returns his look with equal affection. I was with Paul for years and I don't think we ever got lost in each other like *that*. I willingly submit that my place was not meant to be by his side. He eventually found his forever person, and she looks amazing in white.

I look over at Paul's mom and she's beaming as she looks at her son and her new daughter-in-law. Okay, maybe that part hurt a little bit. I've been to that woman's birthday every year for four years straight. I've painstakingly picked out every gift for every holiday and every special occasion; and yet, she hasn't acknowledged me all night!

Whatever. I'm not seeking her approval (anymore).

* * *

When I first received Paul's wedding invite in the mail, I was not surprised to have made the guest list. He was my friend before he was anything else. Before our relationship fizzled out and sent me spiraling into a mess of an adult, I really loved him. And, after I recovered and became less of a mess, I still loved him. I still do. I know the feeling is mutual. Some people are meant to stay a part of your life, no matter how painful some part of that stay may be.

I didn't hesitate to RSVP to the wedding; the plus-one, however, took me a little longer to decide. But when I did, I knew it couldn't be anyone else but him.

* * *

I sit here now at Table Two on Paul's big day. This wedding did not spare any expense. The flowers, the lighting, the wardrobe changes—all impeccably curated. Plus, an open bar? I feel like I should have paid for an admission ticket to be here.

Sitting next to me is a dressed-to-the-nines Cory. He's swaying his head (and parts of his arms) to the bride and groom's first dance song. He's a Bruno Mars fan too. It's one of the many reasons he's my plus-one on this occasion.

I ended my relationship with Paul, tonight's stupidly happy groom, when Cory just entered my life. Cory was there to witness the mess in the aftermath of that relationship. It made sense to have him be my guest tonight to witness the better side of that aftermath.

Cory is enjoying himself and it makes me happy to see it.

We agreed ahead of time that I might go home earlier than him since I am his elder, and I have a set bedtime.

I think it's about that time now.

Cory begins chatting with a few more people whereas I've used up all my social extroversion for the night (I only have so much of that energy to give). I think I've danced enough. It's time to become a hermit again. My bed awaits.

The air outside of the wedding venue is warm. Although I'm wearing a thin, dark blue cocktail dress, the wind feels pleasant against my skin. I take a seat on a bench right outside of the main doors, and let the fresh air take me to my happy place.

My thoughts go to him, and he appears.

Stan's truck pulls up in front of me before I get a chance to take off my heels, which is something I do almost immediately after walking out of any fancy event. It has become customary.

"Let me help you with that," Stan says through the rolled-down passenger side window. He gets out of his truck and kneels to help me undo my heel strap. He looks up at me once both heels are off.

Those eyes still manage to make me feel something. His face is not bad-looking, but his gaze is what captivates me. I wrap my arms around his neck. He pulls me in as he helps me onto my feet. His lips quickly find mine and we kiss. It wasn't a grossly romantic kiss; but it was long enough to convey "Hey, I'm here." This, here—right where he is—that's my happy place.

"Did you get shorter?" he jokingly asks once our lips part. Indeed, without my heels, he easily hovers over me.

He opens the passenger side door. His truck is rather tall, and he insists on hoisting me up every time. Every. Time. It's been like this for the past couple months.

"One day, I will grow, and you will no longer need to do this for me," I say to him.

"I do this for *me*, not for you," he teases.

"I've always pegged you for a creep."

He shrugs his shoulders and looks at me as if I'm not wrong. We both let out a laugh.

Now is probably a good time to tell you that Stan and I are dating. Officially, dating. Being unemployed for the last couple of months has been amazing. (I should have quit a long time ago!). I haven't figured out my career situation, yet (yes, I know that is a major life problem), but I think my personal life is so much better than it was before.

Stan, the droid-like boss, is not the same man as the Stan beside me now. Whatever walls he put up before have long crumbled, and I've learned that his heart beats like a real human man—he has feelings and all!

I'm happy. I hope he is too.

The thing about dating, however, is that neither one of us knows how it's going to end. I suppose that's an obvious fact; we do not know what the future holds.

Sadly, I didn't expect our ending to come so soon—so painfully soon. I am about to be reminded of how fleeting happiness can be.

CHAPTER 24

I sit outside of my favorite cafe as Cory approaches my table. He's dressed in a blue blazer, brown slacks, and flip flops. Business on the top and college party on the bottom? I don't get it, but it works for him. I suppose if you look like a K-POP idol, you can pull off these kinds of outfits. That also applies to anyone under the age of five.

"Hey," he casually says to me.

We fist bump. That is how I greet the younger generation.

"Are you ready to come back to work?" he asks. It seems that whenever he asks me this question, work is the farthest thing from my mind. Cory, however, brings my stressor front and center in the most cavalier way and I'm brought back to reality: I'm in my thirties and unemployed.

"Why do you keep asking me that?"

"I need a friend at work," he quickly answers as if I should have known.

"Why are you still working there?" I ask. "You can clearly afford to quit."

He does his best to look insulted. "It's fun to work for a paycheck."

"When your livelihood does not depend on it," I counter.

He pauses and then nods his head in agreement.

The server brings out our caffeinated drinks. I ordered for Cory ahead of time.

He looks at his drink and says, "Exactly how I like it."

"I know. Milk with a splash of coffee."

He smiles.

"It's gross," I add.

"I know."

He hunches over to sip on his disgusting, poorly caffeinated drink. Why bother using hands to hold up the glass when you can just bring your mouth to the straw?

His eyes dart around aimlessly. I can sense that something is weighing on his mind.

"Say it."

"Okay," he says immediately. He pushes the straw out of his mouth with his tongue and sits up. Then, he leans forward to rest his elbows on his knees. His hands will not stop wringing themselves. He sits back up again and rubs the top of his thighs.

"Enough," I say with a bit of concern. "What is it?"

He leans forward and rests his elbows on his knees—again. "Okay," he repeats. "We are opening up an east coast office of Analytic-Lee. There is a VP operations role available."

"Above my paygrade, but thanks for asking."

He doesn't laugh as he usually does at my poor attempts to make a joke. He's not amused; this must be serious.

"Stan was offered the role," he says.

I can feel my heart begin to race and not for a good reason. I know what's coming next. My body is telling me to brace for impact.

"And he accepted," Cory confirms.

"The job will be remote, right?"

Cory shakes his head.

"And when you say 'east coast' you mean…"

"The opposite side of the country."

"Right." I'm dumbfounded.

I can see he's searching my face for a reaction, but the suddenness of this news is numbing. I grab onto my coffee drink and begin to sip it—slowly. By the time I reach the bottom of the glass and my eyes shift back into focus, I can see Cory is still staring at me intently.

"So…this is what I'm going to do," I say as I put on my sunglasses. "I'm going to walk. That is the most rational thing I can do at this moment. I am an adult. I will think this through. Walking does the body good."

"So does milk. Do you want the rest of my drink?"

"Cory, that really is disgusting."

"I'll come with you. Let's walk together."

I get up to leave. "No, I need a long walk. Judging by how much milk you just drank, you'll just slow me down with bathroom breaks."

"Fair enough."

And so, I walk.

I walk and I feel my chest getting heavier with each step. From behind me, I hear Cory shout, "I can get his job offer rescinded. I know the CEO!"

I would usually laugh at his quips, but I'm having difficulty registering my feelings. Thoughts of Stan take up all of my mental space. Things have been good (maybe too good) between us. I suppose I should be happy for the memories we've made in the time we've spent together, but I crave more.

The tears are starting to well as I'm now power-walking my way towards—well, towards nothing. I'm just walking. I'm walking while a carousel of Stan's images rotates in my brain.

Damn it to Hell, his lovely face. I ignored that face for such a long time and when I finally begin to appreciate the beauty of it, that's when he decides to leave. *Thank you, Universe. Your timing is cruel.*

Walking and crying—I don't want this to become a skill of mine, but it has become a regular occurrence as of late. Walking really helps pump out the tears, especially when I'm trying so hard to hold them in. This is good, however. Let's get all of these emotions out now so that I won't be such a trainwreck later.

Destiny awaits. I have a date with Stan.

CHAPTER 25

I meet Stan at his place for the first time. This date was planned a couple of weeks ago. Had I known *then* that my heart would break *now,* I would have opted for a different location, someplace less intimate. But here we are. We decided to have a night-in at his place.

My hair is pulled back into a loose ponytail to showcase my favorite earrings. Despite my dread and despair, I still managed to make myself look presentable. And by presentable, I simply mean the absence of sweatshirts and jogging pants.

Stan opens the door and immediately gushes, "You look amazing."

He still makes me blush every time he compliments me. It's those eyes. They're penetrating.

I am pleasantly surprised when I enter his impeccably clean home, which is undeniably a bachelor's pad but with the comforts you'd find at a grandparents' house. The bookcases are adorned with well read books, judging by the creases in their spines. There are framed family photos placed throughout the home. A photo of a young Stan and his mother is prominently featured on the side table. *So, that is where he gets his looks; the resemblance is striking.*

I try not to admire this man more than I already do as I take in his home. I remind myself to not get pulled in any farther. Tonight is not about learning new things about Stan (and inevitably loving him more because of them). If anything, I need to start untangling myself from all the comforts that are him.

I feel the heaviness in my chest make an unwanted reappearance. I hate the fact that I'm here. And I hate the fact that his home is so refreshingly clean!

I can feel Stan standing behind me as I continue to stare at the displays on his bookshelves for a little too long. He gently puts a hand on my waist and asks, "Is everything okay?"

"I'm not okay," I let out. I turn around to face him. I didn't want to stumble through a lie, so I went with the truth. Let's be honest, I started my spiral as soon as he opened the door earlier tonight, and now I need to skip to the ending quickly. "I heard about the job offer."

Stan takes a step back from me and leans his body against the back of the couch. He runs his hand through his hair and scratches his temples, clearly more so because of stress than an itch.

"When were you going to tell me?" I ask.

"When I could find the courage to do so."

I'm hurt and I know he can see it on my face.

As if he can't bear to look at me, he drops his head. He says nothing else.

This is the end, isn't it? I feel it in my bones. I see my future changing drastically by the second. The one without him is unkind. My body longs to hold onto him, but I cannot get any closer without crumbling.

"I don't know if I love you," I say, "but I was willing to get there. I was willing to put in the work to get there. I didn't ask for any of this. *You* came to *me*, Stan, and even now I still don't know why you did. I wasn't looking to be…moved, but damn it, I was." I'm pacing and I didn't realize it. "I wanted to see how far we can go, but you've taken that option away."

His silence is insufferable.

Thoughts of Mary suddenly enter my mind. You remember my friend, Mary, right? I truly hope you do; the dead should not be so quickly forgotten.

It's odd how the brain works through an emotional haze. There is Mary, now front and center of my thoughts as I stand here in Stan's home. I get a flashback to our night at the bar.

"Mary used to say that I should hear the way you talk about me when I'm not around," I say. "Had she not mentioned this, I don't think I could have truly believed that a man like you would fall for someone like me. And now, I wish she never let me in on that secret." My despair seemed to have triggered what would have otherwise been a happy memory of Mary.

Stan's face is solemn. He remains silent.

"Stan, you should hear how I speak of you when you're not in the room."

His eyes are locked on mine, but he still doesn't move any closer to me. His lack of words makes our ending seem real and imminent.

This moment is cruel while the silence is loud.

"I'll go," I finally say. I move in closer to him and quickly kiss his cheek. I feel the slight stubble on his face.

I will miss being this close to his skin.

I almost make my way past him if not for his sudden hand on my arm. He holds onto it and gently stops me in my place. With pleading eyes, he asks, "Tell me to stay."

I lean in and bring my forehead to his. When we are this close, it's nearly impossible to resist his pull. I feel both of his hands against my lower back and make their way down to the back of my legs. His mouth finds mine and I allow them to linger there. Like a slow dance, he lifts me up. He carries me into the bedroom as I wrap my legs around him.

I knew—while in his embrace—that this moment will become a beautiful, sad memory.

CHAPTER 26

It's my birthday today. I'm officially smackdab in the middle of my thirties. Hello to popping pills for my joints every day from now on. I never understood the phrase "youth is wasted on the young" until now…now that I'm no longer young. I can no longer get up from a sitting position without my bones creaking, along with other unexpected bodily noises. It's a daily reminder that I'm getting up there in age.

I cannot believe I showed up to work early today. Is this another sign of my age? Have I finally become a committed member of the corporate workforce? No, not really.

I'm back at Analytic-Lee, but I am a manager now. I feel the pressure to do *a little bit* more than the bare minimum these days. It's not as if I have many other things to focus on. I do want to have five babies (I just decided that now), but I need a partner and some really good eggs for that. So, while I'm waiting for my soulmate to magically show up, I figure I should really try at this whole "work thing." Did I gloss over all of that a little too quickly? Let me explain.

* * *

I haven't seen Stan in months. Nine months to be a little more exact. Speaking of Stan, I got his old job position, the one he left vacant after he moved almost three-thousand miles away. I reluctantly put in for the job; Cory, of course, gave me a push. It was between me and John, the guy that broke the office network with his questionable video-viewing habits. I edged him out by just an inch.

Stan. Any mention of his name brings me right back to that night at his place. I can still smell the scent of his bed sheets, a scent that will forever remind me of the end of our relationship.

He left, and I did not ask him to stay. I did not ask him to give up his promotion and stall his career for our budding romance. I could not ask that of him, especially when we were so new. I cannot bear the burden of that decision, which could change the entire trajectory of his life.

I'm okay with my choice to let him go. I do, however, painfully play out the alternative in my head occasionally. It hurts to play the what-if game, but I torment myself from time to time. That probably speaks volumes about who I am as a person. Poor tortured soul.

I might benefit from therapy.

Enough of that. Enough of reliving the moment Stan and I became a love lost. Well, more like an almost-love. Perhaps if I knew for sure that it was love, I would have held onto him as if my future babies depended on it. But as it was, I didn't know then.

I still don't know now.

* * *

So here I am, in Stan's old office. If I were of the weaker mindset, this would be a very hostile work environment. A lot has happened within these walls. But I am surprisingly okay being here. The bigger paychecks also help to overcome this mental struggle. They say money can't fix your problems; I scoff at that sentiment! I'm thriving (despite the occasional mental breakdowns).

Today is my birthday. I need to repeat it so that my mind doesn't wander astray. I know that my birthday means nothing to this company, but I'm going to take it easy today, and that means: a two-hour lunch with Cory.

By the way, Cory no longer works here at this location. He's been working on "special projects" in the east coast office. He used quotes when he told me about his new role there. To be honest, I never knew what he did here (except show up religiously for meetings). He called me last night to tell me he'll be here today. He made it seem like he's flying in just for my birthday; but when I pressed him about it, he's actually here for—get this—a meeting!

I'll take what I can get.

Since we are on the topic of people who no longer work here, Michael is also gone. Michael, the person who made me shout "I quit!" with every fiber of my being. Yes, that Michael. Not too long after Stan got his promotion, which was the same one that Michael was vying for, his ego took a major hit and he decided he needed to go on a "self-love journey." He did, in fact, refer to it as that. Right now, his self-love journey allegedly landed him in a small village in Vietnam where he's fine-tuning his skills in extracting sugar cane juices.

I would have never pegged Michael as someone who needs to love himself *more*, but after our "incidents," I can sense he's harboring some trauma. I was finally able to see behind his good looks and surface charm. He is Sadness walking. Some people are naturally extroverted and magnetic; he is that way for survival.

Here I am, psychoanalyzing someone else as if I have it all figured out myself. I'm a mess. Truth is, we are all messes. Some of us, however, are fortunate enough to have others who can help us clean up those messes or prevent bigger ones from happening.

Here's mine now.

Cory walks in with the biggest smile on his face. It's his default greeting face, one that I've learned to love.

"You're early," I say to him in a deadpan tone as if I'm not elated about the fact that he is three-thousand miles closer to me than he was yesterday.

"Do you want to do a late breakfast, then brunch, and then just continue onto lunch?" Cory asks casually as if it's not a big deal to skip half a day of work. He, as usual, speaks my language.

"Yes. I. Do." I answer while holding in my enthusiasm for the most profound idea I've ever heard. I am ready to eat. Truthfully, when am I not?

Happiness awaits at a breakfast buffet downtown.

The problem with happiness is that it's a series of moments that are in between all of the other stuff. The bad stuff. The heartbreaking stuff. The seemingly broken stuff. It's this other stuff that can easily outweigh the momentary release of dopamine.

After Cory and I ate an atrocious amount of food for the first half of the day, my happiness was at a near peak level. However, I had "stuff" waiting for me when I returned to my office.

CHAPTER 27

M y office." It still sounds foreign when I say it in my head, much less aloud. I worked so hard to get here (if "so hard" means not going beyond my job description), and yet, I'm still trapped within these walls for eight hours a day.

I'm living the dream, aren't I? I still have student loans to pay off and still no house to my name, but I will buy a home one day, retire when I cannot enjoy life anymore due to my declining health, and then leave everything I own to my future children after I die—if I'm lucky.

I don't understand this life.

What I do know for sure, however, is that in my thirty-something years of living, I can only recall a handful of moments that are worth retelling. Here is one incoming.

* * *

It's a little past noon. Okay, I'm lying. I totally took advantage of the fact that I was out with the CEO's son for an extended birthday lunch. It's almost 2:30 PM. Like I said, we ate an atrocious amount of food. I'm well into my food coma and I see someone standing in my office. It takes me about one short breath in to realize who it is.

"Hi, Stan." I say almost in a whisper as I enter my office.

I hate to divert at such a pivotal moment in this messed-up love story, but I must. You've seen those slow montages of the "good times" that usually roll out toward the end of movies, right? Well, I'm having one in my head right now. The moment he looked at me (when he *really* looked at me) from across the conference room table; the moment I felt his lips for the first time; the moment I woke up beside him in my bed. All of those just flashed before me; yet they played out slowly enough for me to relive them in detail. Every. Detail.

It's not fair. It took me nearly nine months to be okay with myself again. I'm okay being alone again. And now, within seconds of seeing him before me, I am wrecked.

He is dressed in tan slacks and a white dress shirt with the sleeves rolled up as is his usual. His hair is neatly combed and freshly cut (no baseball cap today). He looks, well, like how one wants to look when they run into an ex. I, on the other hand, remember how much I ate for breakfast through lunch just moments earlier. I am now painfully aware of the extra weight I'm carrying around my midsection and so, instinctively, I suck it all in.

He looks so good it hurts my eyes. I feel so bloated it hurts my stomach.

"Hi, Sue," he says. I don't remember his voice being so deep. I don't like that I like it. "I had to come see you while I'm here," he continues.

That knot in my stomach is now in my throat. I've thought about what it would be like to see him again, but I never envisioned it taking place at work. I wanted to accidentally (on purpose) run into him after I just finished an imaginary workout at the gym, and I'm rocking some unbelievable six pack abs that are, of course, out in the open for all to see. That is what I wanted. This, right here, is not that. Far from it.

I curse Cory's name under my breath. Of all the days to indulge in gluttony. *Damn it, Cory!*

I stare at Stan, this amazing specimen of a man, and I don't know what my next move should be. Do I shake his hand? Should I go for the guaranteed-awkward high five? (I always miss).

Before I can make a decision, he makes the next move instead. He walks over and gently places a kiss on my cheek.

I cannot explain this feeling that takes over me. I know I will not do it justice in my attempt to explain, but I will try, nonetheless.

His touch did not fuel any romantic flames that might have survived the aftermath of our breakup. Instead, my entire being is consumed with an overwhelming sadness as I look into Stan's eyes. It hits me hard and fast—and all at once. My shoulders feel the weight of this sudden sorrow. It is right here, right now, that I realize I've known love this entire time.

I never knew what love felt like before; I've come close in the past, but I was never certain. As you know, there's no rulebook that outlines all the milestones you must meet before you can call it love. And yet, I am certain now.

It became painfully clear in the simplest way. When flashbacks of our happy moments ended, there was only one thought left that pervaded my headspace: memories are not enough. I could spend a lifetime with *him*, and it'll never be enough. It's an insatiable craving.

My dear readers, I know you may be disappointed that I came to this realization without a dramatic precursor to all of this. No, there wasn't a frantic chase scene to the airport that would end with a confession about my feelings before he forever departs. There was no passionate kiss that brought me to my senses. There was definitely no standing in the rain or any heavy breathing. Cue all those scenes of every romantic movie you've ever seen. There was none of that. Whatsoever. And yet, I will retell this moment for lifetimes. It's the moment I realized that *he* is my forever person. It just took my little brain a little too long to connect the dots.

And now the tears are pushing through. Great. Stan suddenly shows up, barely says anything, and the floodgates open.

He takes a step closer to me and I immediately put up my palm to him. I need an arms-length distance to process my newly discovered feelings.

"No, I'm good." I say as I suck up the tears that have made it down my nostrils. *Embarrassing*. "Just give me one minute and I'll be good. Then we can move onto the next awkward part."

Stan does as he's told. He gives me my space.

Cory suddenly pops into the office with purpose—with fervor! I can almost feel a gust of wind when he enters. He must have run over here; he's out of breath.

"Oh, man! I was hoping you'd be gone by now!" he shouts at Stan. "The meeting ended hours ago!"

I reach out and pull Cory's arm so that he faces me.

"You knew he would be here?" I ask sternly.

I switch from being sad to fuming in seconds. I'm just inches from his nose. I give him the look of death. His eyes frantically bounce around the room to avoid direct eye contact with me.

Cory throws up his hands in surrender as if he knows my wrath is coming.

He's not wrong about that.

CHAPTER 28

To my right is Cory, who is trying his best to not look terrified of me (but he really should be). His eyes are wide and staring directly into mine as if he's frozen; any sudden movement could mean an untimely death.

To my left is Stan, who has just made a surprise reappearance in my life and, consequently, wrecked every bit of normalcy I had going for me.

It's time to smother the internal chaos.

I grab a hold of Stan's hand and lead him out of the office. To my surprise, he interlocks his fingers with mine. The grasp of his hand feels familiar. It almost stops me in my tracks, but I push forward.

I look back at Cory, who cowers at the potency of my stare. He dramatically turns his head towards the window as if a bird (or someone he hopes will come rescue him) suddenly caught his eye. I will deal with him later.

Stan and I end up at a cafe down the street from the office. It's filled with people, but we manage to find a table in the far corner. There's a crowd of customers standing around, waiting for their drink order to be ready. Most of them look like they work in the offices nearby. I can tell by the look of dread on their faces as they wait for their late afternoon dose of caffeine. These are office workers, for sure. Also, their company badges, dangling from their necks and waistlines, are major clues. They are only a couple of hours away from taking off those badges and then actual life can begin again.

I am silently rooting for them from where I sit. We will make it through this day together.

I stop my eyes from wandering and focus them on Stan. His forearms are crossed and resting on the tabletop. He gives me all of his attention with his eyes and body.

"So…" I say. Yes, that's my opener. I thought about it while we walked all the way over here. It's the best I can come up with considering the state I'm in.

"I've missed you," Stan says. *Wow, we are diving right in.* "I've been working so hard; I wanted to see you the first chance I got."

"I thought you were here on business."

"That's my excuse to come see you."

He looks down and starts fidgeting with the watch around his wrist. The watch reminds me of the many reasons why I adore him. I know he's making good money now, but he still wears the same watch his mom gave him years ago.

When he looks up again, I can see the tears he's trying hard to suppress. I'm not sure if it's the watch that conjured up the sad thoughts, or if it's the company at present.

"I'm not the same," Stan says. "I can never be the same after you, Sue."

It's the company at present.

My pulse is racing. I shouldn't be surprised by my reaction anymore; he usually has this effect on me.

The cafe is still filled with bodies, yet it became intensely quiet all of a sudden. It's as if someone turned down the volume in the room and hooked a mic to my chest. The sound of my heart beating rises above all else. The sound is reverberant.

"It haunts me to not understand why you didn't ask me to stay." He looks at me hopelessly with those gentle eyes of his, eyes that could tame a bear. "Why didn't you ask me to stay?"

It hurts me to know that I hurt him. I know the answer to his question—now clearer than ever before—and yet, I cannot find the courage to speak up.

My eyes instinctively scan the room as if I need a quick escape from my own feelings. This man before me stirs up too many raw emotions that I'm ill equipped to handle. It pains me to look at him.

I then spot an oddly familiar older man standing in the crowd of customers. I don't peg him for the usual office worker that frequents this cafe. For one, he's dressed in cargo shorts, a white tee, and sandals. Secondly, he has the biggest smile on his face as he's waiting for his drink amongst the gloomy.

Before I realize I'm staring, he walks right up to our table.

"You are..." he says to me while vigorously snapping his fingers. "You are Mary's friend!" He said it with the most boisterous voice I've ever heard from an elderly man.

It took me a few seconds, and then I remember: he's Mary's neighbor, the butterfly enthusiast. His mannerisms and his voice brought it all back.

"Hi!" I say, trying my best to match his energy level. I fail. I gesture towards Stan. "This is my—"

"I remember you too! The very handsome man at the funeral. You two sat next to each other." Good memory for an older brain. I, on the other hand, can't even remember what I wore yesterday.

"Would you like to sit down and join us?" I ask. Mary would be so pleased with me right now. I'm also reaching for a distraction.

"No, thank you. I'm just picking up some coffee because my energy's low. There's a 'Bugs and Habitats' show downtown that I need to catch. That's why I'm dressed so nicely today." He fashion-models his outfit.

"That's a shame." I say genuinely disappointed. "Next time, then."

He tilts his head down to allow his glasses to slide slightly down the bridge of his nose. He takes in Stan.

"Why so glum?" Mary's neighbor asks.

Before Stan could offer a response, the barista shouts the old man's name at the pick-up window. His name is Frank. I feel that I should have learned that sooner.

"I'm coming!" he shouts loud enough for the entire cafe (and for those walking immediately outside the building) to hear. It was not rude; it was just loud. It made me smile. The confidence to project one's voice is something I admire.

Frank aggressively pats Stan's shoulders and exclaims, "Cheer up! You are too good-looking to be this sad."

He then walks away to get the coffee he questionably needs. But of course, he didn't end our interaction there. From the pick-up window, which is a good twenty feet away, he shouts back to us, "Remember the butterflies!" He guffaws and then leaves.

It is the most endearing exit I've ever witnessed.

Stan and I look at each other and simultaneously burst out laughing.

"I hope that was a decaf," Stan says.

It feels good to laugh through the sadness.

In case you forgot that somber fact: butterflies have an average life span of only four weeks, a measly few weeks to live out a lifetime. It's a reminder that beautiful things will die; moments will fade.

I can't help but think that Mary orchestrated this moment in my life. She didn't know it then, but my knowing her brought Frank into this story, and the timing was perfect. I need more vibrancy and color in my life. Frank brought just that in our brief encounter.

Once Stan and I recover from laughing so much it hurts, he gives me one of his classic Stan smiles—the kind that reassures me he'll be okay. Even when he's hurting, he tries to comfort me. I'm humbled by his kindness. I don't deserve it. He, on the other hand, deserves everything good that comes his way.

I'm thirty-five now. I'm too old to dance around my feelings; I need to own them. If it's love, I should say it.

It's time to tell him my newly discovered truth.

Intuitively, Stan asks, "It's Cory, isn't it?"

CHAPTER 29

It is Cory, the person who has inexplicably morphed from stranger to friend to everything familiar in record time. I know what I need to do with these newly unearthed feelings, but they are too strange, too new, too scary to place them where they should land.

I haven't told him the way I feel about him. After all, it's *Cory*. I tell myself that I will tell him when there's no longer a long line of women vying for his attention wherever we go. You do not know what it's like to be around him, especially at boba shops during peak hours. The attention he receives is borderline fanatical. It's impossible to find the right time to tell him and then inevitably destroy our friendship in one fell swoop.

The pressure.

As it is, I haven't told him that I like being by his side. I haven't told him that I miss him when he's not around. I haven't told him that I love him—that I've loved him this entire time.

Did you see that one coming? Did you know all along that it was Cory? I sure didn't.

What I do know is that I'm not in love with Stan. After seeing Stan again, I don't wonder about him anymore. The what-ifs no longer haunt me.

Stan is one of the most beautiful people to have ever blessed my eyeballs, but I was okay (eventually) without him. I got used to being by myself for the months that we spent apart, and I didn't want to go back to what we had. I didn't realize the state of my feelings until I saw him again, and it triggered a confirmation of my choices.

I know some of you may be disappointed that I'm unwilling to settle for a handsome, successful, humble, kind man like Stan (there's sarcasm in that, by the way, in case you missed it).

I'll be forever grateful for the memories I've made with Stan. They were unexpected and wonderful, but he deserves to make those memories with someone who can return his love with the same grace. That is the thirty-five-year-old me talking. I'm progressing as a human, don't you think? Aging isn't so bad in some ways.

Seeing Stan stirred up some dormant feelings about Cory. Perhaps it was because, prior to unexpectedly seeing Stan again, I spent more than three hours stuffing my face during my birthday breakfast-brunch-lunch with Cory, my favorite person. He was top of mind (as is often the case).

I am myself with Cory. I'm happy with the version of myself when I'm with him—all versions of myself. It's the overly emotional version, the hypercritical-of-others version, the socially awkward version, the just-woke-up-from-a-nap-angry version—every one of those.

I've heard the saying that we are attracted to people who mirror bits of ourselves, but I can't give that saying any credence. If anything, he's better than me. I acknowledge it, accept it, and can admit it.

As if being the better person wasn't enough, he also makes me feel that I am enough. My self-deprecating, negative-thinking self is enough. The weight of his effect on me is unshakable, and I will gladly carry it.

When Stan reappeared in my life after months apart, the sudden emotional exercises wreaked havoc on my tiny brain. The strongest feeling that emerged out of that turmoil was the urgency to run to Cory, my safe spot. It has become a habit to turn to him when I'm in need of comfort and support. He's home to me. I realized it in that moment of seeing Stan again. I didn't ask Stan to stay with me because my feelings for him were not strong enough to hold onto him. But with Cory, home is where he is; I cannot let go.

Just as I thought Cory could not possibly move me any more than he has, he proves me wrong—again. It turns out, he wasn't done making waves quite yet.

CHAPTER 30

I asked her to marry me," Cory says as we walk towards our favorite restaurant for an early dinner.

I stop in my tracks. I suddenly lost my appetite (which is a rare occurrence). Dinner is no longer essential to my sustenance.

I turn to face him with my entire body.

"Who?" I ask while pretending I didn't just get punched in the face with this news. I didn't even know he was dating. Have I been that consumed with myself that I failed to see this coming? Then again, why wouldn't he be dating?

He gives me deadpan eyes. "Becky. I've told you about Becky."

"*That* Becky," I respond. "I thought it was super casual."

"Totally is. But my mom wants me to find someone to give her grandbabies."

"And you thought *Becky* was the best choice?"

He shrugs. "She said 'no' and now I can tell my mom that I've at least tried. I gained a grace period of another year because I'm 'devastated.'" Yes, he used finger quotes.

"How can you be so cavalier about this?" I exclaim. The nerve of the young.

"I knew she would decline my proposal." He flashes me a smile and continues walking.

I catch up to him and make him stop to face me again. "Choosing a partner is no joke. It's one of the most important decisions you'll make," I lecture.

"No, Sue. Choosing *each other* is the most important decision."

Wiseass. How dare he try to out-lecture me? Without saying another word, he continues walking ahead.

I do not budge from where I stand. I watch him walk away, and then he immediately turns around when he doesn't feel my presence following him. We stare at each other from a distance. I fold my arms across my chest and stand up straighter.

I am not moving.

He finally walks back to me, although he's taking his sweet time doing so. When he is close enough for me to see the subtle frown lines on his forehead, he says, "Fine. I will keep that in mind for the next time I propose. She will be 'the one.' Happy?" Again, the finger quotes. His delivery is very convincing.

I shrug. "You know what? I don't care. It's your life."

"Exactly."

"Exactly," I childishly repeat after him.

We remain staring at each other while standing in the middle of the busy sidewalk. I only break my stare when a pair of young women walk past Cory from behind, smiling and turning their heads to get another glimpse of him. I get it, ladies, he looks like he should be modeling his own clothing line.

Cory follows my line of sight and spots the two women as they walk away. They, again, look back at him at that very moment. Little did they know, he would return a smile that would ignite their fandom. The Cory Fan Club has grown, yet again, while he simply exists in public. Insert eyeroll here.

I proceed to walk to the restaurant on my own. He can choose to entertain the newest members of his fan club, or we can resume our plans for an early dinner. Either way, I'm not waiting around for him anymore.

Before I can make it out of earshot, however, I feel his arms around my shoulders, and he begins to power walk alongside me.

"So impatient," he scolds.

I immediately give him an elbow to the side.

As much as he aggravates me, I wouldn't trade this spot right next to him for anywhere else.

He still has no idea that I'm his biggest fan. Truthfully, I'm more like his fan club president.

CHAPTER 31

I t is Friday. It is past five PM. More accurately, it's only ten minutes past five, but when it's a Friday it feels sacrilegious to not be out of the office by four.

It's quiet here. Everyone already left to jumpstart their weekend. They all got the memo that it's a Friday. I got the memo too, but I decided to stick around and finish up my presentation for Monday's meeting. Look at me. I'm putting in overtime—unpaid overtime—and I'm thinking about Monday morning already. The corporate world really got me good.

I supposed I could have spent my morning a little wiser (as in, less people watching from my office window). In my defense, however, it took a while to burn off the brain fog and once I was ready to work, it was already past noon. Some days are just like that. And so, I'm here trying to make up for lost productivity.

I'm not proud of my life choices right now.

Just as I finished adding some amazing animation to my presentation (the extra pizazz really impresses people), there's an unexpected knock on my open office door. It's Angela Lee. She's dressed in her Friday casual fit (which is my Monday best).

She leans on the door frame and says, "Sue, I just wanted to say that the work you've done these few months has not gone unnoticed." She looks around my office, which is Stan's old office. "I'm glad you decided to take on Stan's old role."

I take a few seconds to let that sink in. Then, I take out my phone and say, "Can you repeat that after I hit record? This is really good stuff for my performance evaluation coming up."

Angela smiles. I don't normally impress people with my verbal responses, but I think I'm doing alright with her. Of course, I think to myself whether or not her unprompted compliment is tied to my friendship with her son, but then I remind myself that I'm here past five on a Friday. I'm a great employee. An asset to the company, I dare say! Forget the unproductive morning. I'm still putting in the work.

"Cory was right about you all along," she says. "I forget, sometimes, that he's a great judge of character. I should have known then at the St. Jude's charity ball when he couldn't stop asking about you. I recognize the instant adoration he had—he still has—for you. It makes sense."

Hearing the unprompted flattery certainly brought a smile to my face. There is a brief moment of silence between us. I'm thinking about Cory, and I'm sure she is thinking about her son.

"It's Friday. Go home, Sue. I'm looking forward to your presentation on Monday."

Again, I'm left alone in my office, surrounded by my plants. I redecorated my office not too long ago. The theme: lush forest. I needed the plants to breathe some life into these four walls because, as you know, work is where my soul dies. However, I'm rethinking my design choices as fruit flies are tickling my nose every hour.

I think I may have too many plants.

Wait a minute. As if these plants just reinvigorated my senses, I come to a realization. Did she say the *St. Jude's* charity ball? That specific detail made me stop and think.

You see, our company sponsors a new charity related to childhood cancer every year. St. Jude's was *two* years ago.

I met Cory just last year.

CHAPTER 32

I rush out of my office to see if I can catch Angela Lee before she's gone for the weekend. No sign of her. I need to confirm if she misspoke or not. Details matter here.

The hallways are empty. She is, indeed, gone, and I'm left alone with myself and my confusion.

My mind starts going through my catalogue of memories. The St. Jude's charity ball, which was a couple of years ago, replays in my head in detail.

I remember that night well. I was wearing a long, flowy green dress that fit me just right. It was one of my favorite dresses, one of the very few that made me feel confident in my body. Paul, my ex-boyfriend and almost-fiancé, accompanied me that night. It was the only company event he ever attended with me. The only reason being it didn't conflict with his work schedule. So yes, it was special to me (at least, I thought so at the time). My point is, I remember that night like it was yesterday. Every detail. I would have remembered if I spoke to Cory, or to someone who looks anything remotely like him. That never happened.

The timeline is not adding up.

I call Cory. After several rings, it goes to voicemail. I don't leave one.

I then decide to drop the matter—my overthinking could all be for nothing. I need to stop looking for distractions and wrap it up here at work. It's Friday night, after all. I would like to go home.

About a few seconds in, I get a brilliant idea. Of course, it's not anything related to finishing up my work so that I could jumpstart my weekend of TV bingeing. No, my idea will keep me in this office after hours for way longer than necessary. I decide to go through Cory's social media pages.

An investigation ensues.

One of the first things that Cory shared with me is that he's on social media with a gross amount of followers. "Gross" is my choice of word—not his. I'm more of a private person who, in general, does not like people. So yes, "gross" seems like a fitting description to describe the number of strangers who know too much about you. It doesn't surprise me, however, that Cory would amass such a following. That face should be a national treasure.

I admit, I never looked at his social media profile before. That's mainly because he is always around. Physically. In real life, in real time. So, I never had a need to look him up…until now.

Bam. There he is online. He wasn't hard to find at all.

I'm scrolling through his photos with purpose now. There are photos of his tattoos (some I know of, some I didn't). There are photos taken of many events. *Many* events. My social anxiety is flaring up just seeing him in his full-fledged social butterfly form. Restaurant openings, bachelor's parties, pottery classes.

How are we even friends?

I slow down when I reach the photos from about two years ago. As suspected, he posted photos for the St. Jude's charity ball. He was, in fact, there that night.

I scroll through more pictures from that night. He posted photos of the food, the people dancing, the décor. And then I come across a less lively photo, one of a long hallway just outside of the main event space. There is only one person in the entire frame. Although she is not the center of the shot, she is distinguishable even in the dimly lit space. She is walking out of the grand ballroom as she's holding up her long, flowy green dress.

That's always been my favorite dress.

CHAPTER 33

I call Cory again. He picks up this time. It's noisy on his end.

"Where are you? I ask immediately.

"Hello to you too. I'm at the Italian bistro downtown," he says.

"I need to see you. Stay there." I hang up without further explanation.

I don't have a clear plan; I just start walking. The restaurant isn't far from where our office building is. I can get to him in less than ten minutes. Work can wait. I need some answers now.

I run the last twenty steps as I get closer to the restaurant. I'm so glad I'm wearing my casual Friday outfit. It's just shy of wearing sweatpants at the office.

When I'm almost at the restaurant entrance, I see Cory walking out of the double doors to meet me outside. I bend down to rest my hands on my knees. I'm winded. I just sprinted the longest distance of my life.

"Is everything okay, Sue?" he asks. I hear the concern in his voice. He's a little more dressed up than I'm used to. This is clearly not his Friday casual.

"Hi." I finally greet him. Then I jump right to it. 'When did we first meet?"

"At work."

"Be more specific."

"At work. At your desk. It was a Friday." He answered so quickly, it seemed rehearsed.

I shake my head while still trying to catch my breath. I take out my cell phone and show him the photo—the one he took of me at the charity ball without my knowing.

I watch the happiness drain from his face. The change in his expression is swift. His lips are pressed tightly together. I seem to have hit a nerve. He tucks his hands into his pockets and gently asks, "Can we talk about this later? Now is not a good time."

He nudges his head towards the restaurant window. I look over in that direction. There's a woman—a very attractive woman—sitting in the booth alone. She is staring at us with laser focus and furrowed brows.

It takes me a few seconds to read the scene. He's on a date, one that I'm in the process of interrupting. When I make the connection, my face turns bright red. I feel it burning with embarrassment. Of course, he would be on a date right now! He's dressed up on a Friday night at a restaurant. Major giveaways.

"Call me when you can," I say. "It's not urgent."

The excitement and enthusiasm of solving this mystery is completely gone. I feel like an idiot.

Cory doesn't say anything. I see it in his eyes. It's like he's reliving a painful memory. I regret taking him down this path. Sad Cory is my least favorite Cory. What am I doing? I was looking for a distraction from work and now my favorite person looks at me like I just punched his dog.

Well, the damage is done. I will leave him as he was—on a date. I look back towards the woman in the window. Yes, she's still staring.

I think I'm done here.

I slowly walk back to the office building where my unfinished work awaits. The streets always seem extra lively when I cannot take part in any of the downtown Friday night activities. Life's tease.

It's a lovely warm evening with an occasional breeze. Perfect walking weather to clear the head. Except, not *my* head. I cannot turn off my brain from overthinking.

Why did Cory look so sad when I showed him the picture? I want to know what thoughts entered his mind upon seeing that photo. How did he know me before we ever met? I was expecting a simple explanation—something along the lines of a matrix-like time warp mix-up. Something like that. But his reaction tells me it's much more complicated.

Again, I don't have a clear plan, and so I walk.

I continue to walk as I try to make sense of what just unfolded. I don't get too far, however, when I feel a tap on my shoulder. I let out a scream. It was sudden and loud. I wasn't aware that anyone was walking behind me, much less expected to be touched. In hindsight, the scream was a bit too much in response to a tap on the shoulder, but it was fitting for what I thought was a monster trying to eat me.

I turn around. The monster is Cory. I want to punch him in the gut. Of all people, he knows that I get scared easily. But it's Cory being Cory. He just pops out of nowhere.

He doesn't look any less sad than when I left him earlier.

"I met you at work, at your cubicle, on a Friday afternoon," he begins. "I will never forget when I first met you, but I will also never forget the moment I first *saw* you.

I tune out the sound of my own breathing. I tune out the sounds of downtown. I wait patiently for him to say more.

"I was at the bar talking to this guy I just met," Cory says, "and all of a sudden, he looks off in the distance and stops talking completely. Literally mid-sentence. I look at what he's looking at. It was you, Sue. In a green dress."

He waits for me to respond, but I say nothing.

Cory continues, "I, of course, had to ask about you. Stan had nothing less than kind words to say. You should hear the way he speaks about you to other people, Sue. You are his favorite topic."

"Stan?" I ask. I heard him, but I didn't trust myself to hear him correctly.

"Yes, it was Stan at the bar," he says. "I don't think he recognized me from that night when we met again, but that's not surprising considering what a distraction you were for him."

"Stan?" I ask again.

"Yes, Stan! That Stan. Your Stan. I don't know if you know this, Sue, but he was in love with you," Cory says sarcastically.

I, of course, know that now.

"After seeing you for the first time, I was…intrigued." He finally smiles at me. "The way that Stan spoke of you, it made me wish I knew you myself."

I'm processing what he's saying. Should I be flattered or angry? I don't know which emotion I'm leaning towards, but the prevalent one is confusion. Second runner-up is disbelief.

"Was meeting me contrived then?" I finally ask.

"A little bit? I did mention you to my mom. I told her I had a good feeling about you. And maybe I let it slip that I was infatuated by you and that perhaps one day you'll have my babies." He says that all in one breath. I hate it when I cannot tell if he's joking or not.

Again, I feel the urge to punch him in the gut. At the same time, I'm hanging on to every word.

"What is your long game, Cory?"

His smile fades and the earlier version of him returns, the somber version. In a serious tone, he says, "I've just been waiting."

"For?"

His eyes soften. "For you to choose me, too."

If this was a movie, this would be the scene in which it suddenly rains, and we continue to stand here—like idiots— getting completely soaked unnecessarily. You can visualize it, right? Tonight, however, the sky is clear, and the only idiot is yours truly. If there ever was a perfect moment to tell him how I feel, I completely squandered it.

Instead, I say, "I don't think I'm going to finish my work tonight."

He replies, "I don't think I'm going back to my date."

CHAPTER 34

We are finally here. If I could pin any moment in my life that mirrors the peak of a rom-com movie, this would be it. Cory, dressed in his date night best for someone else, tells me that he wants me to have his babies (essentially, that's what I hear even if he didn't use those exact words). As a woman in her mid-thirties, my ovaries are exploding with joy upon hearing this. Couple that with my feelings for him and I immediately turn into goop. As expected, I cannot get my mouth and brain to connect in such a pivotal moment as this.

A very solemn Cory looks at me as if he needs to reach out and hold onto something for support. I want to be that for him, but I'm not confident that my knees won't buckle.

"Sue, I find you"—he hesitates—"fiercely attractive."

For the record, I've never been described as such by anyone, ever, until now. The closest I've come was when a boy in junior high school called me "weirdly attractive." It doesn't carry the same weight, does it?

Cory continues, "When you were about to get engaged to Paul, I thought that was it—I lost my window. Then the engagement didn't happen, and I thought here's my chance, finally. And then—"

"Stan."

"Yes. Stan." He lets out an exasperated sigh. "Who can compete with a man like Stan? Even I get weak in the presence of his gorgeous face. I don't know how you resisted for so long. I mean…"

I give him deadpan eyes. "Weird tangent."

"You're right." He takes a moment to regroup. "Sue, I've waited patiently. And in my waiting, I've grown to love your laughter, your quirks, your sarcasm, your thoughtfulness—all of which comes in this package of a beautiful person. You're almost too much."

"*You* are too much!" I instinctively respond like a defensive child. I never imagined these words would ever come out of Cory's mouth. If it was anyone else, I would listen with caution; but it's Cory, my friend for when the rest of the world scares me or ignores me. Trust comes easily with him. I'm listening with every fiber of my being. He deserves that at the very least.

"I don't expect anything from you, Sue. You should know that. I don't need anything more from you than what you're willing to give, and whatever that is, it's more than enough."

I know he's trying to neutralize the situation and keep me from running. It's working.

"I'm a patient man," he adds with a wink. Classic Cory, always trying to lighten the mood.

I forget that we are in the middle of a busy sidewalk. It's downtown on a Friday night. People are passing us left and right while we stand in their paths like lost tourists (or entitled sidewalk hoggers). I usually don't like crowds, but the hum of downtown nightlife lightens the gravity of our conversation. I appreciate these strangers, a sentiment reserved only in dire situations.

With groups of people buzzing by, I'm reminded, yet again, of the amount of attention Cory receives while just existing. I see their eyes lock onto him as they slow down their pace to let their gaze linger for a little longer. Gone is their sense of urgency to get where they needed to go.

"So," I begin slowly, "what did you tell your date before taking off like that?" I know that my question has nothing to do with what he last said to me, but this is the progression of my thoughts, which has jumped all over the place tonight. And with these onlookers noticeably present, my thoughts wander to Cory's date.

Without any hesitancy, he says, "That you're my cousin and there's a family emergency."

"That's going to bite you in the ass later."

"Probably." He nods. "That sounds fair."

I smile because of the unadulterated honesty in his answer. I have no doubt that he told his date exactly that.

"You know that we look nothing alike," I say.

"Thank God!"

And *that*, my dear readers, is how we ended that conversation. One that started out emotionally packed ended on a lighter note that allows us to continue as we are: friends. That's the power of Cory. The extent of comfort and ease to which he makes me feel is unmatched. It also helped that we ended the night with a stop at a burger shack.

Food is comfort. And so is Cory.

By now, I think it's clear that Cory is the leading man of my story. I think I did enough foreshadowing all along, did I not? He's changed my life in ways that are equivalent to life events like getting a puppy or signing up for a timeshare. Life. Changing.

I will keep his newly revealed feelings close to my chest. I will treat Cory's love like the life of a butterfly, as if it will end at any moment. After all, all good things must end.

And *that* is some more foreshadowing indeed.

CHAPTER 35

Monday is here again. Every week, it immediately follows Sunday and yet, it sneaks up on me every time. I thrive on the weekends when I'm living my best life, and then Monday shows up and ruins every desire I have for greatness. Mondays are my kryptonite (or perhaps my excuse). At least it keeps me humble.

Today is the day of my big presentation. I'm dressed in my best pantsuit, one that screams middle management with a side of extra potential. I feel confident. That is, until Cory walks in, and I freeze up.

"What are you doing here?" I ask.

He takes a seat in the front row. "To root you on, of course."

I should have figured that he would be here. Attending meetings is in his job description, which is strangely still a mystery to me.

Before I could process Cory's unexpected attendance, in walks Stan. Cory immediately gets onto his feet.

"What are you doing here?" Cory and I say at once to Stan. Cory sounds just as surprised as I am.

Stan walks in with two cups of coffee in hand. He hands me one. Cory, standing in between the two of us, watches this gesture as if it's a sports replay.

I watch Cory watch Stan.

"Some of the east coast managers are here for another meeting this afternoon," Stan says. "I figure I could sit in your meeting and learn from you."

I nod. "Of course." And then I quickly add, "It's good to see you."

Cory moves swiftly to reclaim his seat in the front row. Stan takes a seat right next to him, a little off center in the room but still prominently in front of me. I could almost picture the two of them subtly fighting over the armrest. Then again, I don't need to imagine it—they are, indeed, subtly fighting over extra elbow room. Predictable.

Well, this is a strange start to my day, which I thought I would conquer with confidence. After all, I worked so hard on my presentation, which is complete with stunning clipart and mind-blowing nineties graphic animations.

And now, I have the two biggest distractions in the room.

More people are filing in. It's time to put on my professional pants and turn up the work vernacular. I will wow.

I wowed indeed. By the end of my presentation, Angela Lee (more commonly known now as Cory's mother) wanted to implement my ideas as soon as possible. I will save you the boring details of the content of my presentation (it had to do with automation of data extraction and cleansing). Aren't you glad I spared you the gory details? The point is, I wowed while effectively compartmentalizing all that is non-work related, namely, the two gentlemen who crashed my meeting.

As the team begins to shuffle out of the conference room, I tidy up (which means I simply close my laptop)—and I keep my back to the room as I stall for everyone to leave. I take my sweet time winding up my charger cable.

I finally turn around when I feel the room is empty.

Wrong. Stan's face is so close to mine that I'm sure he can count the cells on my nose. I can count his. When he is this close to my eyeballs, my brain reminds me of how attractive he is. He looks like he walks around with a photo filter on, except his beauty does not turn off.

"Walk?" Stan asks.

Out of nowhere, Cory puts his arms around both Stan and me. "That sounds great. We should all go!" Cory exclaims.

I didn't realize that Cory was still in the room. Stan took up all my visual space with his face so close to mine that I didn't notice Cory until now.

Cory flashes me a smile. I return a look that tells him to behave. He answers that with an even flashier smile.

"So," Cory says, "where are we going, Stan? Never mind, I know the perfect place to go to clear our heads."

"Why does your head need clearing?" Stan asks.

"It's filled with bad ideas," I say.

We—the three of us—make it outside. The mid-morning crowd downtown is probably my favorite. Those who are frolicking in shops at this hour make me wonder what they do for a living. Those who are outside holding half empty coffee cups while checking the time every few minutes are dreading the end of their work break. Or perhaps I am projecting. Perhaps some people are, indeed, content with their work and with the hours they put into it. I, on the other hand, want to put in minimal effort and get paid the most. The more I move up the corporate ladder, the more I believe that this can be less of a pipe dream.

Cory leads the way. We end up at an open stairway located to the side of a busy outdoor food court. At first glance, it looks like the stairs will lead you to the office building above. By the time we reach the top, I realize it leads to a rooftop garden instead. There are many of these in the downtown area. They are perfect for when you want to eat lunch in peace, or when you want to have phone interviews without your current employer knowing. (I'm speaking purely from observation). This particular garden, however, is new to me.

It's empty up here at this time of day.

"Is this where you plan on killing me?" I ask Cory in a serious tone.

"Your sense of humor has always been"—he gives his next choice of word careful thought—"unique."

"I accept that assessment."

He chuckles. "If killing you was my plan all along, I wouldn't have invited a witness." He gestures towards Stan.

"I'm uncomfortable with this conversation," Stan says.

We smile at each other and then we all turn our attention to the view. From up here, I see our office building located a few short blocks away. The Grand Hall, where the annual charity ball takes place, can also be seen from here. If I squint hard enough, I may be able to see my small apartment complex that sits on the edge of the city.

We stand in silence as we take in the view. Cory's to my left and Stan to my right. This is peace, but it is quickly interrupted by Stan's next words.

"I'm moving back," he says.

Cory and I almost snap our necks as we immediately turn to look at him.

Stan's eyes are squarely focused on mine as he adds, "For work."

It's so quiet that I can hear the sound of my own eyelids opening and closing. I understand that blinking rapidly doesn't allow me to hear any clearer, yet this is how my body chooses to respond.

Stan continues, "I'm taking over Michael's old role…with some restructuring."

"You accepted the job?" Cory exclaims.

"You knew about this?" I exclaim in return.

"I didn't know he accepted the job."

"That's partly why I'm here," Stan says. "I'm meeting with your mom to discuss the new team structure."

"Interesting," Cory says slowly. "*Very* interesting."

I see Cory's face change from amused to concerned in a matter of seconds. The wrinkles between his eyes are in full form. As for me, my eyes are still stuck in rapid blinking mode and my expression is one of disbelief. And Stan is, well, familiarly expressionless. His face is relaxed; no facial lines to indicate where he may stand on the spectrum of possible emotions. He does, however, keeps his eyes on me regardless of Cory's heavy breathing.

Cory could be convulsing right now, and Stan may not notice.

Once my eyelids are done exercising, I extend my arms and give Stan and Cory a pat on the back as I inch backwards away from the lineup. This has been an exciting Monday so far, but not the kind of excitement I want this early in the morning.

"I'm headed home for the day," I say casually.

Before I could stop myself, I was already firing finger guns at both of them as I backed away. Again, I don't know why my body chooses to react this way. Never count me out when it comes to making a situation more awkward than it needs to be. I'm reliable in that way.

I start to make my way off the rooftop, but of course I turn around before I descend the stairs. I see Cory and Stan facing each other against this picturesque backdrop of the city skyline. Their lips are not moving, but their stances say a lot. This standoff may last a while, and I'm not interested to see it to the end.

Another Monday for the books. I have this theory that the week will (usually) end the way it started. It's similar to when I put in my contact lenses in the morning, and they don't feel quite right; it's an omen that the day ahead will be unpleasant, just like the speck that's rubbing against my eyelids every time I blink. If you know the feeling, then you know—it's a minor pain that will consume your energy and ruin your day.

Today is that speck in my eye. By Friday, I will need serious help.

CHAPTER 36

Angela Lee sent out a memo for an all-hands meeting. She usually refrains from having company-wide meetings, so you can imagine the amount of talk swirling around the office in regard to this one. The all-hands is scheduled for Friday at four PM. Daunting.

It's Friday today, and the time is 3:45 PM. The anxiety that precedes this meeting is relentless. Will this meeting bring news that will render me jobless, or will it invigorate me to work harder? I'm leaning towards the former.

Very few things here make me want to work harder. I earn every paycheck. To work harder means I should be compensated more. It's unfortunate that companies have not caught on: valued employees value money over any other company "perks." Perks don't pay rent. Retention is in the compensation. And if an employee walks away from more money, then it's time for the company to look inward at the managing party. I'm sure I've said this already: employees quit their boss, not their job.

I digress.

I'm nervous. I'm wondering what I will eat for dinner tonight while also wondering if this weekend will be filled with tears or not. This meeting is disrupting the end-of-the-work-week vibes.

I wait (the right amount of time) before I head over to the conference room. Showing up too early to a meeting means small talk. Showing up too late, well, that's never good.

It's 3:57 PM. Time to head over.

To my surprise, Stan is at the front of the room right next to Angela. What is supposed to be their Friday casual looks more like Monday business. I don't like how their power suits make me feel.

"I'll cut to the chase," Angela says. "Our company has undergone some changes. We had to let some people go." A collective gasp fills the room. "If you were invited to this meeting, then you were not one of those people."

Safe. For now.

The rest of the meeting was filled with buzz words like "synergy" and "efficiencies," which is code for downsizing. By the end of it, I learned that my old boss and once boyfriend, Stan, is now the manager of a new position that would oversee my team and two others. In other words, a few managers got the boot, and the teams are now consolidated under Stan. The main takeaway: Stan is my boss again.

I'm sending out S.O.S. signals as I look around the room for Cory, who is nowhere to be found. His absence is concerning considering his affinity for meetings. Perhaps *he* is the one in need of help.

I send him a quick text.

He responds, "What meeting?"

Oh, no.

CHAPTER 37

I start my weekend off thinking about work, which is *the* worst way to jumpstart my weekly two-day vacation. It's Friday night and I'm grabbing dinner alone at a quiet restaurant on the edge of the city. I plan to fill myself up and then wobble my way home. I don't have many options this Friday night. Cory is not picking up my calls, and my mother is busy. Table for one, it is.

I'm mid-bite when my phone alerts me that I have a new message. It's from Stan. It reads:

Can I join you?

I quickly look up and scan the room.

There he is at the entrance of this small restaurant. I must not have been hard to spot.

"You're not hard to spot," Stan says, echoing my inner thoughts out loud.

It is now that I realize my mouth is still half open. I quickly put down my fork. That bite can wait.

"Was this a coincidence or you knew I was going to be here?" I ask.

"I knew," he says. "We used to date. I know your patterns."

The mention of our past dating relationship makes me uncomfortable, especially now that he will—once again—be my boss. Sitting here in this dimly lit restaurant across from him will be a red flag for human resources.

The waiter comes by and asks Stan what he would like to order.

Stan turns to me. "You're not expecting anyone here, are you?" he asks.

I shake my head.

"I'll have exactly what she ordered."

"I ordered two entrees," I say to him.

Stan smiles. "Yes, one for later." He turns to the waiter. "Same."

He remembers me all too well. My discomfort is mixed with nostalgia. I suppose they cancel each other out. I *should* feel nothing, but I unwillingly do.

I shift in my seat. I'm not sure what I'm supposed to do next.

I try not to stare, but it's hard to pull my eyes away from Stan. I look at him and wish him nothing but happiness. I normally reserve such wishes for the less physically blessed, but he deserves it (despite his freakishly superb genes). He's a beautiful human inside and out.

"Should I order a bottle of wine?"

His question snaps me out of my one-sided staring contest.

We spend the next hour catching up and laughing (and drinking). Turns out, Stan despises the east coast weather. He misses the blended seasons of California. I tell him new experiences are good for him. He tells me I know nothing about what's good for him. The point is, we are comfortable. This is easy.

After we cover just about every minute detail of how we spent the last nine months since our breakup, we finally talk about the changes at work. And of course, talk of work inevitably turns into talk of us.

"Why did you seek me out tonight?"

"I wanted to do exactly this. Catch up," he says. He then flashes a playful, almost sly smile. It's not like him; it must be the wine. "My hotel is also just a block from here. This is convenient."

Well played, Stan.

"Can I walk you home?" Stan asks. I might have imagined the wink he didn't give me, but a wink seems fitting considering the energy. This is progressively getting too playful, or it may all be in my head, which is far from clear right now.

We walk. I appreciate the company home. It's a chilly Friday night. I feel it more intensely as the wine works its way through my system.

I stop suddenly and face Stan.

"I demand your jacket. I will not give you subtle cues that I am freezing in hopes that you will offer your jacket. We are past that. I need your jacket, old friend."

He seems very amused judging by his smiling eyes. However, he doesn't move. And then suddenly he does (and it wasn't to give me his jacket).

I didn't see it coming. I didn't expect any of it.

All I feel are his lips on mine. I feel his kiss so intensely as if it's the only source of warmth available. This feels familiar and yet so different.

I take a step back from him. I must.

"I'm sorry. I don't know how to stop loving you," Stan says.

I could blame the wine for his sudden behavior, but his eyes tell me it's a nonfactor.

It seems that the Universe is trying to double down on Stan and me. Why else would it let this man before me deliver such a line like *that?* It's so passionate, it's unkind.

Stan has moved me before, and I'm in awe at how easily he can do it again. However, as much as the ground may give way, I know where I stand. My heart hurts for him. My heart hurts to hurt him.

"But you need to stop," I say, barely audible. And with that response, I can feel his body cave in.

"I know," he says softly. He leans his forehead against mine.

I gently place my hands on his cheeks, holding his face between my palms. I pull my head back to meet his eyes. "Stan, you're not missing out on much here."

I give him my best smile. He does his best to return one.

Stan lets out a long sigh. "I'm leaving tomorrow. The next time I'm back—"

"You'll be my boss again," I finish for him.

"Right."

We stand in silence as we let that sink in.
"But until then…" he says with a wink.
This time, I know I didn't imagine the wink.

CHAPTER 38

Stan walked me home that night and then he walked back to his hotel—alone. The playful energy from earlier in the evening dissipated by the time we got to my door. It was a sobering walk home, but we both needed it. The walk gave us time to reflect on our newly found circumstance. Reflection made it easier to say goodbye that night.

The rest of the night, however, was far from over.

I wake up to the sound of my phone ringing. I check the time. It's almost one in the morning. My body wants to roll over and go back to sleep, but I pick up because it's Cory.

"Can you open the door, please?" he asks quietly. The somberness in his voice is obvious. It wakes me up immediately.

I rush to the door.

Cory stands in the doorway. He doesn't move, he doesn't speak, but his posture immediately gives off defeat.

"What's going on?" I ask.

He falls into me—completely. He leans against my body as if his entire being just gave up. I hold him up with all of me, doing my best to keep the both of us from toppling over.

Once inside, I can see that he's been crying and drinking (always a terrible combo). I feel his pain instantly; I feel it in my bones. I want to completely absorb whatever trauma is weighing on him if it means that I can see his smile.

And there it is. Completely forced, but he tries his best to give me a smile to ease my worries. Unbeknownst to him, it worries me even more.

I hold onto him. I don't know what to say in this situation, but I know that physical touch can be more comforting than words. I run my hands through his hair as he lays his head on my chest.

"It's my mom, Sue," he finally says.

He doesn't say more, and I do not press him. And so, we lay there in silence, with him wrapped in my arms, on my tiny couch, until the morning.

CHAPTER 39

Cory's mom has been battling cancer for years. Stage four pancreatic cancer. Cory thought the battle was coming to an end, but apparently, chemo is no longer working. Surprisingly, no one at work has a clue that she's undergoing any treatment at all.

Angela Lee is always poise and exudes power. The juxtaposition of Corporate Angela and Cancer Patient Angela is hard to visualize. And those organizational changes at work? Well, leave it to Angela to get everything in order before she steps down. Preparations made under those circumstances are unfathomable.

All of this was conveyed to me via late night rambling.

I woke up early today. I slide into the side chair next to the couch as I watch Cory sleep off last night. My dear Cory. I want to kiss his eyes to settle the thoughts that cause his eyelids to flutter in his sleep, but I stop myself. I'm afraid he's too delicate to touch.

"Stop looking at me with pity," Cory suddenly says with his eyes still closed. It's early and he's already inside my head. He sits up and looks at me with half-open eyes.

"It's hard not to when your shirt is tear-stained," I say.

"That's drool." He gets up and frantically looks around. "I came here with a jacket, right?"

I point to the wall where it's hung. He goes over to get it and then suddenly comes back towards me. He kneels in front of me so that we are eye to eye from where I sit. He looks at me intensely, as if he's searching for his soul (or for his keys) in my eyes.

"Thank you," he says. He gives me a gentle kiss on the cheek. "For not taking advantage of my vulnerability last night."

I slightly push his chest. It is apparently strong enough to make him lose his balance. He grabs hold of my arm and inadvertently pulls me down with him. And of course, just like a rom-com, I land on top of his not-surprisingly-firm body. However, there's no awkward reshuffling of our bodies here; there's no big gasp at how we ended up in this predicament. He proceeds to simply wrap his arms (and legs) around me—bear hug style—and hold me captive.

It's nothing romantic; it feels more like a trap. Or perhaps, it's more like therapy. I hear a long, exaggerated sigh escape his lips and I realize that it is *his* therapy; he needs this.

"It's not too late to take advantage of me," he says. Those words do not match the tone of his voice. I see the tears form in the corner of his eyes. I know that he is using humor to cope with the news about his mom.

Everything about this moment hurts me.

"I'm going to get off you. And you will go find your mom," I say to him.

He lets go of me and my bones feel immediate relief, although my body aches to be held like that again. It's a good kind of ache.

I walk Cory to the door. He reluctantly walks in front of me and almost makes it out of my tiny apartment. Just as he is about to open the door to leave, he turns around and slides his arm around my waist. Unexpectedly, he pulls me in and kisses me. The softness of his lips takes me by surprise. Our lips touch gently, and slowly, and with intent.

When we finally part, he says, "I'm sorry."

I will, soon enough, understand the weight of those last two words Cory said to me.

CHAPTER 40

The weekend, as always, came and went, and I'm already back in front my computer lifelessly checking emails. I'm finding it difficult to focus on work, so I redirect my (lack of) energy into watering my plants to death.

The fruit flies are now gone; it seems they have given up as well.

I kill another five minutes by staring aimlessly out of my office window. As usual, I wonder if there is someone in the window directly across the street from me, who is doing the exact thing I'm doing now. I am tempted to wave, but it might signal a sign of distress.

I need to get some work done.

I turn my body back towards my computer, but my eyes immediately gloss over the tiny black text on my screen. Every fiber of my being does not want to do this today—this whole "working thing." I've never missed my bed so much. Perhaps I'm feeling unwell.

I lay my head down on my desk. I just need ten minutes. I will rest my eyes and then I will start this Monday off right.

It was after lunch by the time I saw the sun again. It's unbelievable that no one walked into my office during my deep slumber and woke me. It's also uncharacteristic of me to not care if someone saw me in such a state at work. It's not a good look, but right now, I don't have the energy to care.

I feel exhausted from life.

I slowly become alive again when my nose catches a whiff of a savory aroma. It's a familiar smell. It takes my senses a few seconds to recognize it. It's chicken noodle soup, and it's sitting on my desk with a note.

> You look terrible.
> Go home and rest.
> - Cory

Brutal honesty. So, someone *did* catch me dozing off at my desk. I wish Cory would have woken me up, but I will accept the soup and go home.

I get up to stretch and I immediately feel the need to sit back down. My head is spinning, and my face is numb. I'm a grown adult and it took me half a day to realize that I am, indeed, sick. It wasn't just the Monday blues that got me today.

I quickly pack my things and groggily make my way out.

I pass by empty cubicles and offices. It's too quiet here for this time of day. This is odd. Even the breakroom is vacant. *Where is everyone?*

I then pass by the big conference room, the one with the glass sidings, and I see the entire office convened inside. That is, everyone but me. Leading the meeting is no other than Cory. And beside him is no other than Stan.

In what universe did I accidentally cross over?

I walk slowly past the conference room. Very slowly. Slow enough for Stan to make eye contact, and then for Cory to do the same. Cory continues on with the meeting after he gives me a slight nod from afar. Stan, however, leaves mid-meeting and meets me outside.

"Are you planning a party for me in there?" I ask once we were out of everyone's eye line.

"Yes," Stan says in a serious tone. "Are you okay?" he asks in an even more serious tone. His face frowns with concern.

"No, I'm not. I must be sick to have missed the memo for this meeting." I then remember that he doesn't work here—yet. "What are *you* doing here?"

"I'm back—for good."

Before I could process the suddenness of this news, out pops Cory. Just like that. Out of thin air he appears. This has become a skill that he's honed to perfection.

He steps in front of Stan. Their shoulders make contact with each other as he moves forward to speak with me.

"Do you want me to take you home?" Cory asks me.

The question made Stan glance at him sideways. Cory's tone, however, is stern; there is no gentleness in the way he offered to take me home. It felt like an obligation, and I, a burden.

"No, I'll walk," I say somewhat unconvincingly. I do not want to walk, but I don't want him to take me home either. I am no one's burden. "Did you just leave a meeting full of people?"

"I told them it'll just be a second," he replies casually, as if it's not a big deal to walk out on a room full of people who are there in the first place by his request.

I lean my upper body back slightly to peek into the conference room. Yes, everyone sitting in there is staring in our direction, as expected when the presenters walk out in the middle of a meeting.

This has been a weird day. My body is not feeling well enough to make sense of this odd pairing that is Cory and Stan. They are both staring at me as if I'm a fragile butterfly. I don't like it. The intensity of their stares is a little too much when I'm in this state of sickness.

I'm going home. Right now. And so, I simply walk away, not bothering to say my goodbyes to either of them.

As I'm almost at the exit door, I look back, expecting both of them to head back towards the conference room to the audience they abandoned. Wrong. Cory and Stan, both dressed in collared shirts and slacks, continue to stand there and watch me leave. They simultaneously wave at me. The energy is…weird.

Somehow, I made it home. As soon as I walk through the door, I plop myself down onto the nearest soft surface I can find. My body is ready to morph as one with my couch and go into shutdown mode. I will deal with today, tomorrow.

CHAPTER 41

Tomorrow turned into a full-blown week of coughing, sneezing, wheezing, dying, and being reborn again. Half of the office came down with every sickness under the sun. We all eventually reemerged from a cloud of vapor rub and menthol.

When I finally reenter the office after my unplanned week-long sick vacation, I find that someone had moved into the office adjacent to mine. That office was left vacant by Michael, who, according to the latest office rumor, is still on his self-discovery journey on a remote island somewhere in Southeast Asia. I hope he gets the peace he's after.

Back to the vacant office. There's now a laptop and a chair residing where Michael once sat. No nameplate nor office signage is present to give a clue as to who my new neighbor is.

The mystery is quickly solved, however, when Stan walks by with his head in his cellphone. He miraculously makes it into the office and onto his seat without ever looking up.

"Hey," I say ever so casually as I lean against the door frame of his new office.

He finally looks up from this cellphone. "Welcome back."

"I should say the same to you. Cool digs." As soon as "cool digs" left my mouth, I immediately regretted it.

He gets up and gives me a hug. I stiffen up. Are we allowed to do this? We are navigating new waters here, and I don't know how volatile it may be.

He senses my hesitancy and immediately backs away with both hands up.

"That was a strictly professional hug. It did not conjure up any old romantic feelings about us. At all." He tries to smile at me convincingly. His smile doesn't do its job of convincing me of anything other than we both don't know how to be normal at the office (whatever "normal" means).

After our brief awkward pause, I open my arms as wide as they could go. "Come here. I am glad you're back on this side of the country. Welcome back, *Boss.*"

"Boss," Stan repeats. He nods more to himself than to me.

"We don't need to go way back to the days when you barely talked to me and couldn't remember my last name," I say as I gently pat him on the back.

"You mean the good days?"

I inadvertently let out a cackle. I think Stan and I are going to be okay. If we can share moments of genuine laughter after all that has transpired between us, then we will be alright. After all, we are both highly functional adults, one being more obnoxiously attractive than the other. How can this *not* work?

Change of subject is needed here.

"Have you seen Cory?" I ask.

"He's gone."

"To?"

I apparently didn't read the company memo in between my vomiting and being heavily medicated during the week I was out. The memo addressed the changes to come, including remote work, closure of the east coast office, and other cost-savings initiatives. Cory is assigned to a two-month project to wrap up business at the company's other offices.

A change in work life is not something I will complain about. After all, we can continue to grow and expand as a company while working from the comforts of home. Cory being gone for two months, however, is not something I look forward to.

"Shouldn't you be there too, Stan?"

"I need to oversee the team here while the rest of management is there."

I look around. Suddenly, it already feels very different here.

"Do you wish that I'm over there instead of Cory?" he asks me bluntly.

I give that some thought before I answer, "No."

We are all where we need to be right now. I'm ready to get back to work and rebuild this working relationship with Stan. And Cory, he needs to be with this mom and spend as much time with her as possible.

CHAPTER 42

I haven't heard from Cory since he left. His two-month project turned into three, and now going on four. While it's been hard to adjust to not having his seemingly ubiquitous presence in every facet of my life, it's even harder when I have no idea how he's doing. The swift and dramatic change in our relationship has left me feeling lost. And perpetually hungry (he usually comes bearing food).

I've been productive, however. I play Solitaire only twice a day while I cram four hours of work into two. Every day, I challenge myself a little more. Tomorrow I may try to cram eight hours into three, play only one round of Solitaire, and then go home early.

I do miss Cory, however, regardless of my impressive productivity rate.

I'm working hard to mask the fact that I'm hurting. Not a single text from him. Not a single email. I would settle for an indirect social media post, but everything of his has gone dark.

He must know that news about Angela's condition has made its rounds, and I imagine the pity-stares and preemptive condolences he receives because of it. I understand the need to shut down and to become laser focus on something—anything—other than *that*.

Selfishly, I want him to slow down and come back into my orbit, but I know that he's coping in his own way.

It's simply dreadful that he's not here. I just want to reiterate that point.

Onto more important news.

The office stopped offering free coffee. I'm not mad about it. Ever since Mary's passing, I've never looked at that carafe the same way.

Mary. I think of her, and I want to go home now. Life is too short to be an overachiever at work. I cranked out three reports today. It's practically an office record. I should be out in the streets celebrating my accomplishment. I don't know why I need to be "out in the streets," but it paints a picture that I must be unconfined from my corporate cuffs.

I gather my things to leave, and then I'm reminded that Stan, the chronic workaholic, is right next door. I quickly glance at the wall clock. It's two PM. I can justify my leaving at this time, or I might not have to at all. Let's see how this goes.

I casually stroll past his office door, which is always open lately. "Bye, Stan," I say as soon as I'm out of his view.

"Sue," he calls after me. Calling my name from his office reminds me of the beginning of our relationship when I would try to minimize all facetime with him. It's difficult to believe how much I avoided him before, especially now that I fully recognize (and appreciate) the beauty that sits on his face and the kind soul that he is.

"Heading home?" he asks when I enter the doorway.

I nod. He smiles as he looks at the wall clock. We are both well aware of the time of day.

I say nothing and smile back.

"Get home safely," he simply says.

I should count my lucky stars and be grateful that my boss recognizes my hard work and lets me escape the office early. I should head straight towards the exit and enjoy my afternoon freedom.

I should. But I don't.

"I'm going to get a post-lunch lunch."

"Classic Sue."

"Any chance you want to come?"

There's a short pause. A very short pause, but just long enough to know that he had to think about it.

"I could use a second lunch."

He's a changed man! The Stan I knew before would never skip out of work early, not even when we were dating. He is a creature of habit as we all are, but he is more (annoyingly) rigid than others.

So, off we go. Just me and my ex-boss slash ex-boyfriend slash boss-again. What could go wrong?

CHAPTER 43

We end up at a bar downtown. Stan suggested a nicer restaurant closer to our office, but I convinced him to go here, which is a much better match to my credit limit.

Bar food is so underrated, anyway. I'm fine with waiting twenty minutes for a basket of piping-hot fries made by the sole cook in the back. There is never any sticker shock here, even after I eat to my heart's content.

Two baskets of fries later, the happy-hour prices kick in. It's time to buy my boss a drink.

"It's been really nice working with you again." I raise my glass. "To good bosses."

"To friends."

"To good friends." I will drink to that.

In between our drinking, eating, and laughing (which are all the good things in life), the topic of Cory comes up and sadness begins to creep into the atmosphere. Stan gives me an update on how things are progressing with the closure of the east coast office. I listen to every detail with a heavy heart.

I'm tempted to call Cory at this moment, but my ego cannot handle another straight-to-voicemail scenario.

"What happened between you two?" Stan asks bluntly. "Did he propose, and you rejected him?"

"No! Why would you assume that?"

He shrugs. "It's obvious that he feels a certain way about you—it's hard not to."

I'm not sure what to say to that, so I go with, "We are just two weirdos who are friends."

"Can I give you some advice?" he asks more so out of politeness than for permission. "Take it from someone who loved you for a long time. You, just being you, is tough to be around. Not knowing where you stand makes it hard. You are all-consuming and you don't even know it."

I'm convinced Stan should be the leading man in a rom-com movie. Agents should be scrambling to represent that face. It's *that* face and *those* eyes, coupled with his honest vulnerability, that set the bar for swoon worthy.

I contemplate his unsolicited advice. I then put my arm behind him and give him a slow pat on the back. "You are delusional, and that's okay."

He lets out a cackle. I haven't heard one of those in a long time. It's right up there with snorts. Cackles and snorts are some of the best sounds to ever escape our mouths. They are so unabashedly unexpected; it's beautiful when it happens.

This must be a sign that Stan and I are doing just fine. Our relationship has progressed into the kind that allows for shame-free bodily noises to make an appearance every once in a while. It's healthy and wonderful.

Then, unprompted, I say, "I won't be coming into work tomorrow. There's something I need to do."

CHAPTER 44

It is the anniversary of Mary's death. I marked her death on my calendar before I ever marked her birthday. What a twisted order of events.

I place the freshly cut flowers over her tombstone. The vibrant yellow petals are a stark contrast to the early morning fog.

I feel a tap on my shoulder. I cower as I let out a high-pitched shriek, the kind you might expect a goat to bleat in its last moment of life. I just unlocked a new decibel. To be fair, I am at a graveyard; it is reasonable to think that I was just touched by a ghost.

I reluctantly turn around (very slowly), and I see a somewhat familiar face staring back at me. It takes me some time to summon the name that belongs to said face. To my astonishment, it's Michael, my old manager, the one who made me quit my job because he was a vile, unlikable man.

He might as well have been a ghost. No one has heard from him in almost a year. And here he is now, in the flesh, with longer hair, tanner skin, and more accessories than any one man should adorn at once.

"I didn't mean to scare you," he says.

"Then don't sneak up on people who are standing alone at a gravesite!" My heart is still racing from the sneak attack.

"Fair enough," he acknowledges.

"What are you doing here?" I ask as I glance around vigorously for a potential eyewitness. Can you blame me? I don't know what his agenda is.

"Same reason you're here."

"Fair enough," I conclude. And then I add, "But why?"

"That's a fair question."

"It is."

This conversation is quite intriguing, isn't it? We are treading carefully.

I watch him as he contemplates his answer. His unruly blonde hair and sun-beaten skin do not take away from his perfect bone structure, which annoys me to admit. In this morning fog, on this dreary day, his face still radiates and captivates. His prettiness is unwavering (and unfair). Lucky him.

"I worked with Mary for over ten years," Michael says. "When Mary passed, I was too much in my own world to care. It sounds terrible, doesn't it? It sounds terrible to say it; I'm sure it sounds worse to hear it. I was too self-absorbed to care about the passing of a human being."

He pauses for a moment, as if he's hearing those words out loud for the first time and he needs to process the weight of that sentiment. He drops his head and focuses his eyes onto his feet.

"Yes, you were an asshole." I say pointedly. This news should not surprise him.

"I deserve that." He lets out a long, frustrated sigh. "Mary didn't deserve it though. Mary had to deal with assholes like me who felt the need to overpower and stifle those around me due to some defunct superiority complex."

"Wow! Self-awareness is odd on you."

"I know it's jarring. I'm still working on myself."

"Then you should start by getting rid of that seashell necklace."

He takes a step back and looks at me surprisingly. "Wow, where was this fire back then?"

"It was stifled by your superiority complex."

He bites his bottom lip as he tries to suppress a smile. He nods his head in agreement, then drops his head in defeat.

"I've always liked you, Sue."

"Oh, here we go!" I say as I roll my eyes dramatically.

He puts up both hands in defense. "I just want you to know that I'm sorry for my behavior. It wasn't you. It was me—obviously. I have many 'complexes' to work through."

He doesn't know it, but I forgave him long ago. I cannot harbor resentment for someone who, I know, was hurting before our paths ever crossed. On the other hand, I also think hurt people still need to be accountable for their actions. And so, I will not consider Michael a friend (far from it), but I'm willing to start at square one.

"We are past it," I simply say.

His smile tells me that it is enough (for now, at least).

The air just got noticeably colder. Michael rocks back and forth on the ball of his heels. The silence is strangely comfortable as we both stare into the space in front of us.

"I was never happy with myself." Michael suddenly stops rocking back and forth. "I was always chasing something that could bring me closer to feeling like I'm enough. Daddy issues, I suppose. Whatever. I couldn't find contentment."

He glossed over that last part a little too quickly. I'm self-aware enough to know that I'm not the person who can help him heal from that. I decide to lighten the current mood, especially considering the scene. We are literally standing in a graveyard. The mood is already "grave" as it is (ba-dum-bum).

"Well, you came to the right place!" I give him a heavy-handed slap on the back. He almost falls forward but catches himself.

He looks around at our surroundings. Confused, he says, "The right place is at this place of death?"

I gesture towards Mary's tombstone. "Mary told me that you can trick your brain into being happy." I turn to face him and pinch both sides of his cheeks. "So, fake a smile and laugh." Even with his face distorted by the pull of my fingers, he is still nice to look at. "Try it. Now say 'ha-ha.'"

"Ha-ha," he says through clenched cheeks.

"Ha-ha-ha." I say, one-upping him.

"Ha-ha-ha-ha." He's catching on.

I let go of his cheeks and his smile forms on its own. "Ha-ha-ha-ha-ha!"

This goes on until we reach about a dozen "ha's." By the end of it, we are both laughing hysterically. This rudimentary dialogue is the best conversation we've ever had. Here we are, two grown adults, laughing uncontrollably in a place that permeates sadness. I imagine that if anyone were to stumble upon this scene, we would look like raging lunatics. Albeit the happiest lunatics this cemetery has ever seen!

I wipe away my happy tears and my mind goes to Mary. Even after her death, Mary continues to facilitate moments like these in the lives of those who knew her. I owe her for these happy tears, these much needed, unexpected happy tears.

When the hysterics die down, Michael and I simultaneously let out a long, relaxed sigh. I can now hear the sound of my own breathing, a stark contrast to the boisterous laughter just moments ago.

Michael suddenly looks over at me and says, "I can see why Stan was always so fond of you." His smile is gentle, and his eyes are earnest as he lets out that unexpected compliment.

I feel my cheeks redden after the mention of Stan's name.

He continues, "You should hear the way he talks about you."

I let out a long, exasperated sigh. "So, I've been told," I say slowly as I look up at the gray sky. Is the Universe trying to tell me that I made a mistake for letting him go? Stan, is he the one that got away?

A car door closes in the near distance and the sound snaps me out of my existential crisis. The sound reverberates in the expanse of the cemetery.

Michael and I look towards the car. Cory, dressed in all black, gets out of the back seat. Even in this dark scene, he shines.

My questions for the Universe are answered as I watch my favorite person make his way towards us. His smile—however slight—is a beacon.

Michael squints as he tries to make out the figure in the distance. "Is that—"

"Cory," I say just above a whisper.

I must be seeing ghosts, after all.

CHAPTER 45

I'm afraid to move. I fear that if I do, Cory will disappear again. I didn't know that I was holding my breath until Michael gave me a hearty slap on the back and I found myself gasping for air. To which, Michael responds with additional slaps on the back—this time, firmer—to resolve the choking that his first slap induced. All well-intentioned slaps, but I need him to stop helping me.

"Are you okay?" Michael asks.

I'm not okay but I give him a thumbs up while the oxygen slowly makes its way to my brain.

I am clearly not okay. I haven't heard from Cory in months and now he's in front of me.

When Cory reaches us, Michael extends his hand and excitedly asks, "Remember me?"

"Can't forget you," Cory responds cautiously. They shake hands.

"Remember me?" I ask Cory solemnly.

"Can't forget you," he says. They are the same words he had just spoken to Michael, but the delivery is drastically different. There are layers there, and it gives me hope.

I can't take my eyes off Cory; he's like a rare unicorn (yes, I said "rare unicorn" and I know it's redundant).

He hasn't taken his eyes off of me either, but it's giving less rare unicorn vibes and more I'm-concerned-about-her-well-being vibes. This is fair considering I was just gasping for air only moments ago.

Michael, who I forgot was standing right here, darts his eyeballs back and forth between Cory and me.

"I feel like you two need to talk. I will get back to my chickens," Michael says.

I decide to table my questions about his chickens for later considering the current energy. But trust me, I have questions.

Michael literally gallops away.

And then there are two.

Cory places flowers on Mary's tombstone. Soft yellow flowers.

The sun begins to peak through the morning fog that just started to dissipate. As usual, Cory brings the sunshine wherever he goes.

I start with the basics. "How have you been?"

"I'm sorry," he says instead of answering my question.

I shake my head as if the last four months didn't break me the slightest. It did and it still hurts, but I do not let him in on that fun fact. And so, we stand here in the deafening silence as we stare at Mary's name inscribed on her tombstone.

This is the first time that Mary, Cory, and I have been together since that day at the bar, that day when Mary drank us both under the table. Missing today, however, is the unfiltered laughter, the kind that derives from the pits of the belly. This is not the kind of reunion anyone hopes for.

"Cory—"

"I should get going," he says suddenly. "My driver is hungry. He gets 'hangry' like you do."

Just as abruptly as he showed up, he leaves in the same fashion. I watch as his hungry driver drives off with purpose. I'm then left alone in this graveyard with only my thoughts.

I don't know which is scarier—this cemetery or the thoughts that take up my headspace. I decide that it's this cemetery, and that I should leave before another ghost appears.

This is the loneliest I've felt in a long time.

CHAPTER 46

There are very few moments in my life when I enjoy getting dressed up. This isn't one of them, but I still make the effort. It's the company's annual charity ball. This year's charity: American Childhood Cancer Organization. This year's event spared no expense on the elaborate décor and fancy food. Like every year, the party's façade covers up the ugly behind cancer. It can't cover up the fact that this year, however, we know that our CEO is fighting a battle of her own. The turnout is up compared to previous years. The sign of respect is not lost in the number of attendees.

Last year, I came to this event with Cory by my side. I had a literal support system that I could lean on in five-inch heels. This year, I'm wearing a sparkly gold dress with flats—fancy flats, I should add. I plan to focus my efforts less on *not* tripping and more on devouring as many appetizers as possible before my sit-down meal. I have goals for tonight.

Five minutes in and I already have a plate full of goodies. I casually walk and eat (it's amazing how easily I can multitask in comfortable footwear).

There are a lot of familiar faces here; small talk abounds. My mouth is busy chewing, however, so most people are satisfied when I simply offer a smile. It's either that, or wait for me to stop chewing, which admittedly, is going to be a long wait.

I spot Stan from afar. As usual, he is dressed for this event; the tuxedo fits him well. He must have been one of those babies that came out of the womb wearing a tuxedo instead of a birthday suit like the rest of us. He looks natural in his fancy form. And like every year, he matches his neckwear to the event's cause. His gold bowtie is an endearing touch to his formalwear.

I refill my plate of hors d'oeuvres.

Truthfully, I'm hoping to see Cory at this event. We haven't spoken since the run-in at Mary's gravesite, which is not the place to unpack the last few months. There will be no unpacking done at tonight's event either, but I'm looking for confirmation that he is at least okay (as okay as one can be in his situation).

I find a seat at an empty table. Most people are still walking around and mingling while I'm already waiting for dinner to start.

I do not plan on getting up for the rest of the night.

There is static over the PA system, followed by a loud voice. "Everyone, please find a seat. Dinner will start promptly at 6:30. But first, a message from Analytic-Lee's owner and CEO, Angela Lee."

People's heads are moving left and right as they try to see where Angela may be. I get up onto my feet as soon as I see her center stage. I will stand for this.

Our brain chemistry is a curious thing. When armed with new information, the way we *see* a person can change. Angela Lee was never a frail person in my mind's eye, but after learning about her cancer battle, she seems measurably delicate even though she looks the same. Whatever efforts she made before to hide her condition, she is still putting forth now, yet I cannot unsee what my brain logically thinks I should see: a fragile cancer patient.

After reading the room, Angela says, "Now, don't look at me like that. I'm not dead, yet."

Everyone is on their feet. The pain behind that joke is not lost on the room. My eyes well up.

"I'm sure the news of my," she pauses briefly, "*failing body* has made its way around the water cooler. Let me remind you, I still authorize all your paychecks."

We smile through our tears.

"I'm kidding. Your paychecks are too small for me to authorized."

Laughter erupts.

"Tonight is not about me, however. We all know why we are here tonight. The reality behind these lavish events is that cancer treatment costs more than an entire family's income in some cases. Can you imagine having your child go through treatment while worrying about the bill? Can you?

The tears are now forming a small pool on the top of my crossed arms.

Angela Lee continues, "I know that the ticket prices for our annual event are exponential. But"—she holds out one hand—"childhood cancer"—she holds out the other—"or an overpriced night of dinner and dancing?"

The room is quiet. You can hear the sporadic sniffling of those whose tears made their way down to their noses (me included).

"And remember, for every ticket sold, the company does a one-hundred percent donation match, so stop your boo-hooing."

The silence is replaced with a steady build-up of clapping and some whistling.

"I want everyone to raise a glass. Let's remember to enjoy the mundane, the routine, the ordinary. Love who you want to love. But more importantly, love out loud. If you don't speak it, it doesn't get a chance to manifest. We are all fighting our own battles, so enjoy the process. Life is short."

"Life is short," I repeat under my breath.

Angela walks off the stage to rapturous applause. I'm assuming there is not a dry eye in the audience. If there is, those people are dead inside.

That was a poignant and humbling speech. Her words weigh heavily on my heart.

I look for the nearest exit. My initial plan of stuffing my face in the name of gluttony tonight is now replaced with a desire for a quiet night in the comforts of my own home.

I want to go home to *my* mundane, *my* routine, *my* ordinary.

I feel a hand on my arm as I turn to leave. It's Stan. I inadvertently let out a laugh when our eyes meet. Terrible timing, I know.

I mentioned earlier—that thing about brain chemistry and how our view of people can change after knowing a detail about them. Well, that whole train of thought reentered my mind as I look at Stan's kind face. It's the same face that I avoided for so many years, but when I got past the robotic boss facade, his face became new to me. It was a paradigm shift, and I can no longer unsee what was unseen before. Again, the laughter is bad timing and, admittedly, confusing if you are on the receiving end of it.

I give him my best comforting smile in hopes to undo my unseemly laughter from earlier. I'm doing my best to convey to him that I am stable (enough, at least).

He returns a smile that pierces through my black heart. I put my hand to his cheek and say, "I'll see you Monday."

I turn to walk away, but I suddenly stop myself. I feel compelled to tell him, "You are loved, Stan."

He then gives me a smile that could revitalize dying crops. That face is a work of art and should be considered in negotiations for world peace. My point is: he deserves someone who can love him openly and honestly. I want nothing less for him, while I wish for him the world.

I walk into the empty hallway outside of the main venue. It's starkly quiet here. As soon as the door closes, the liveliness of the party in the next room is stifled, leaving only the sound of my own breathing to reverberate off the walls.

I take my time as I walk down this grand hallway and listen to my footsteps, each one creating a unique sound that will never be heard again. The echoes are bigger than me; they give life to this dimly lit hallway. I feel a burst of confidence knowing little-ole-me can cause so much noise, even if no one is here to witness it.

"Hello!" I shout to no one. I listen to the echoes of my voice move slower and farther away from me. "Hello!" I shout again. I wait and listen. *Why is this so much fun?*

"I'm here," says a voice from behind me.

The echo makes its way closer to me and I feel the hairs on my neck stand up. And then I see him in the distance.

He truly has a knack for showing up out of nowhere and invading my personal space.

CHAPTER 47

I listen to the sound of Cory's footsteps as he makes his way closer to me. He's dressed in an understated black tuxedo—simple and formal. This dimly lit grand hallway is a backdrop to his own personal runway. He radiates as he consumes all of my energy immediately.

If this encounter was under different circumstances, we would embrace, and fireworks would go off in the distance. Sadly, it's a very different scene from where I stand.

Let the awkwardness ensue.

Should we fist bump? Maybe I'll let him make the first move.

No, I then decide that he needs to be pushed instead. And so, I push his shoulder, hard enough to make him step back to regain his balance.

"I gave you space, but instead, you jumped galaxies," I say to him.

A slight smile forms at the corners of his mouth. He says, "That is almost poetic."

We then proceed to stand in silence, just like we did the last time we were together. I vividly remember the empty feeling that consumed me after he left me alone in the cemetery. Being left in a cemetery, of all places, can be brutal; I don't recommend it. I wish to not be left by him ever again—in a cemetery or any place, really. That kind of emptiness should be short-lived and never relived (if we can be so lucky).

My mind is bombarded with words that I want to speak, but I can't form a clear thought. Let's just go with the obvious first.

"I missed you," I finally say. "A lot."

"Me, too. A lot."

We both let out a heavy sigh.

"You know, don't you?" I ask.

He furls his brows and tilts his head in confusion.

I continue (before I lose the courage to do so), "You know that in the next few minutes, I will tell you that I love you. Let's just set the scene. I will tell you that I miss you so much it hurts. Whenever I stub my toe on my bedpost, I curse your name. When I find an amazing sandwich spot, I tell myself that I need to take you there one day. I find it endearing that you claim to drink coffee when it's mostly milk. I also think it's gross."

This isn't exactly poetry that I am spewing, but it'll have to do. Bear with me.

"You know, don't you?" I ask again. "You are home to me. You are where I feel the safest. I like to share my airspace with you, and that says a lot considering my aversion to people." I look down at the ground and take a deep breath in. I'm finding it difficult to convey my intentions clearly. When I finally look up again and meet his eyes, the right words suddenly flood in and fill the void. "I choose you, Cory. I've chosen you a long time ago—I just didn't know it then. I will choose to choose you again and again."

There, I said it. I put it out there in the Universe and those words can land where they may. Those words, which cannot be unspoken, will forever live within this hallway and in this moment as I watch my favorite person hear them for the first time. The delivery could have used more eloquence, but the message is all the same.

I, in my mind, pass the microphone to him.

But Cory remains silent. His smile is gone. His eyes are softened by the tears that are forming in their corners. I see his shoulders drop as he exhales for what seems like the first time since I started my impromptu monologue.

I suddenly feel so hollow. I can tip over by the slightest gust of wind.

The doors leading into the Grand Hall abruptly open, and the silence is interrupted by the sound of the party in the adjoining room and of guests shuffling out. I can no longer hear the echoes of their footsteps when there are too many colliding in the same airspace. I don't know if I prefer the silence or the distraction. Both hurt just the same.

Cory shakes his head as if he's shaking off bad thoughts. He squeezes my hand and slowly lets go.

And then, I watch him walk away. I watch the outline of his frame get smaller with each step until he completely disappears from my view.

I am no longer hollow; I am completely empty.

I was wrong, my dear readers. As it may, being left alone in a cemetery is not brutal; it seems almost kind compared to the silence in the presence of someone you love.

In the end, there is no embrace. There are no fireworks. I go home alone to the mundane, to the routine, to the ordinary.

CHAPTER 48

I'm taking a week off from work. It is Monday and I'm starting my unplanned vacation now as I lay here in bed with no agenda for the day. You may think that I'm trying to avoid seeing Cory again. You may think I'm in need of some "me" time because I'm utterly broken and completely embarrassed.

You would be correct.

I will cry the ugliest face imaginable until this feeling of devastation passes. I have some amazingly intense crying faces. You'll just have to take my word for it. I do not document my tears; I prefer to do my crying in private. (I cringe at those who post videos of themselves crying. The ick factor in those videos is so much that it burns my eyes).

Sadness should never be used for social currency, and that is a hill I'm willing to die on.

I give myself a week to get through all the ugly crying. And if that isn't long enough, I have more vacation time to burn.

But first, coffee.

I roll out of bed and somehow got myself onto my feet in record time. It must be the momentum from the fall. It wasn't a roll; it was a fall. I definitely fell. In my haste, I stub my big toe against my bed post on my way to the kitchen.

"Damn it, Cory!" I shout to the ceiling.

And the ugly crying starts.

So, this is my life now. I'm in my mid-thirties, no kids (not even a pet to cuddle with), and I'm crying way too much over a hurt toe (clearly, a displacement of emotions). This is how I should describe myself on dating sites: "Stable until toe gets hurt." That's accurate.

I decide to forgo the coffee. There's no need to add caffeine; it'll only elevate the crying to new levels. Besides, there is no need to get out of bed. I am on vacation. Let entropy amplify as I find comfort in the only consistently stable thing in my life: my bed. All else can digress into chaos.

My doorbell rings. Of course, my plan of having *no* plans is interrupted as the Universe has different plans for me.

It's Stan.

Now, as lovely as his face may be, I categorically find it unsavory to see my boss on my vacation time. It is so wrong; I should be compensated for the emotional and mental duress that spawns from his presence. I should also charge by the minute for this unscheduled visit. My overtime rate could possibly buy me a new heart. It is no secret that I'm in need of a new one.

"How can I help you?" I ask. I am even surprised at my inability to hide my annoyance.

He must be preoccupied with other thoughts for my tone went over his head. And then I see it in his eyes. I recognize the look of pity, and I don't like it.

"You missed all my calls." He looks at me up and down. "Why are you still in your pajamas?" Stan asks.

I look down at my attire. Indeed, I am still in my pajamas at—I look over at the wall clock—a little after ten-thirty in the morning. I understand how the image of a grown woman in unicorn-printed pajamas may incite pity. Then I remember that I am on vacation. I don't plan on wearing anything else. I bought these pajamas in bulk.

"Stan, I am on vacation."

"No, you are not."

I look at him as if he just grew a unicorn brow (yes, singular). "Excuse me?"

"Your vacation starts *tomorrow*. I delayed your request for time off by one day because you have a presentation scheduled for *today*. I called you—many times—to preview your presentation deck. I came here thinking that something horrible may have happened to you." He looks at me up and down again. "But you look…like you are on vacation."

This is the moment that I experienced my first outer body experience. It is me who is standing in this room with Stan. I look down at this grown woman—in her amazing pajamas— who just forgot about the presentation that she worked on for the last two weeks. Her jaw is on the floor. This is not me. I may not be good at many things, but I am GREAT at working. So how did I get here?

The obvious person to blame is Cory. You were thinking the same, right? No? You were thinking that *I* am in charge of my own destiny, and that *I* should be more responsible?

Well, that sounds fair.

I put my hand on Stan's shoulder and give him my best game face. "Did you drive here?"

We make it to the office in record time. Stan drove through downtown without hitting any pedestrians, which is a feat considering we were nearing lunchtime, the part of the day when crosswalks look like little ant farms.

I walk into the conference room at exactly 11:15 AM. It's enough time to set up and stand there looking poised, as if I've prepared for this all morning.

I'm dressed in my Monday best, tailored black slacks and a white blouse, in hopes that it will convey confidence. I *am* confident, I remind myself. I know my material and I stand behind my numbers. I can compartmentalize my thoughts of Cory and put on my work persona. This should be a walk in the park.

But of course, as soon as I start believing in my self-affirmations, in walks Cory. This is like a cruel joke in a movie I don't want to see. However, I should have expected this; Cory loves meetings.

I watch him without watching him as best as I can. Instead of taking a seat in the front and center of the room, Cory slides into the very back—the farthest distance from me. He crosses his arms and leans against the wall. I cannot read his face clearly from where I stand, but it may be for the best.

I have a job to do. I will not let him derail me at work. It is best not to look at him. I'll table all things Cory-related for tomorrow, when I restart vacation and the ugly crying can continue. Until then, it's work and nothing else. After all, I am a professional; I can keep up this persona for the rest of the day.

He was the first to leave. As soon as I completed my presentation, I watch Cory walk out the door before the applause was over. He didn't hang around to ask me to grab a two-hour lunch (not even an extended coffee break). Admittedly, that hurt. But at the same time, he owes me nothing.

CHAPTER 49

The dread of coming back to work after vacation is real and heavy. That is a very sad fact of life. I even dread the dread that inevitably comes when vacation ends. It creates a big black hole in my heart where happiness and energy go to die.

And just like that, I am in the office again. It's clearly too soon to be back as I'm immediately overwhelmed by the plethora of neglected plants that surrounds me. I've just sat down, and already, I don't want to be here anymore. It smells like death in here. The smell of rotting plants makes me want to roll over, as well.

I recall how I spent my precious vacation days couped up in my apartment. Some people may not be able to spend that much time alone, but I relished it. No makeup and pajamas all day is happiness in the simplest form. On the other hand, it was time spent away from seeing the one person who heavily influenced my decision to spend time alone in the first place. But the space from Cory was needed. It was time well spent—mostly on my bed and on my couch, tucked away under soft comforters where I was able to cry in peace. And that, I did.

I must have been deep in thought when Stan walked into my office. I didn't notice him until he called my name.

"Sue, are you okay?" he asks. His tone is soft, but I can see the frown lines on his face.

"In general? Never," I say bluntly. *Does my appearance give him reason to be concerned?* I quickly check my reflection in the window. I nod to myself. I'm decent. I should be proud that I even put on my work pants today.

I look straight into Stan's eyes (and into his soul), and then I say casually, "I shouldn't tell you this because you are my boss, but in all honesty, I don't plan on doing any work today. I'm going to slowly reacquaint myself with the *concept* of working again. It's probably going to take me until the end of the day." I continue to stare at him blankly.

The gentleness in his eyes does not fade. He smiles, which brings some life back into this room. At this point in our relationship, I find comfort in the ability to spew honesty this easily. I do not take it for granted. I hope the feeling is mutual.

Neither of us say anything. The moment has turned into an unspoken game of who will blink first.

He does.

And then I see the frown lines reappear on his flawless face.

I feel my stomach suddenly drop. My inner voice tells me that I may not like what he's going to say next.

"You haven't heard, have you?" he asks softly.

I wait for him to continue. My breathing becomes more rapid, and I feel my muscles tense up along my spine. My body is apparently responding to the stress and anxiety of news that my ears haven't even heard yet!

Stan's face is telling. *This cannot be good.*

"Cory quit," he says carefully as if those words can break me. Well, they did.

CHAPTER 50

Let's try this again. My extended vacation starts now. Upon hearing the news of Cory's departure, I had more ugly crying to do, and I would like to do it in the privacy of my own home.

So here I am again, under the covers in bed, and trying not to think of Cory and all of my burning unanswered questions.

The problem is, my mind won't turn off. Once my eyeballs get a glimpse of sunlight, my brain wants to download and replay all the tragedies that I fell asleep to last night. Those unanswered questions are now keeping my eyelids wide open.

It's terribly annoying.

I get up—unwillingly, as you may imagine—and I do the *one* thing that I know I shouldn't: I engage in some social media scrolling. Considering the state that I am in, I should brace myself for the spiral of self-criticism and endless comparisons that await me at the end of this rabbit hole. And yet, I jump right in.

Someone, help me.

My eyes are inundated with photos of family vacations, babies, and endless post workout selfies. I'm not jealous; I'm envious. I learned that there is a difference between the two. Jealousy is feeling *threatened* by what someone has, whereas envy is just wanting what someone has; their happiness (at least what is shown in these photos) has nothing to do with me. I just wish I could take a decent selfie once in a while to show the world (all of my 200 internet friends) that I got it too. But, damn, those angles are hard to master. The lighting is never kind to me either.

I'm casually scrolling through these photos as if I'm not deliberately hoping to come across one of Cory's. I am, of course, and I tell myself to stop.

And so, I stop—temporarily, at least. I need to eat. Envy can get ugly on an empty stomach (as does most things in life).

When I get back to my bed, and back onto my laptop, I nearly choke on my half-eaten cookie. Yes, you read that correctly; I chose a cookie for breakfast. It's a crunchy chocolate chip cookie at that, so imagine the crumbs everywhere. Before you pass judgement, let me remind you that I am on vacation, and I am still reeling from Cory's sudden departure from work.

Back to the reason I'm choking on cookie crumbs.

My social newsfeed updates, and at the very top of my screen is a picture. It was taken in a dimly lit hallway. I don't immediately place the location, but I recognize the sparkly gold dress, which stands out against the dark background.

That's *my* sparkly gold dress, the one I wore to the company's last charity event. I recognize myself in the photo, which is captured just as I stepped outside of the grand ballroom. I am alone. My expression is not clearly discernable, but I remember the feeling all too well as I left the party that night—I missed my friend and I desperately wanted to go home.

Unbeknownst to me, Cory captured this moment. It was the moment right before I told him I loved him, followed by immediate regret the size of the space between us.

It was in this dimly lit hallway that I thought I lost my friend—the friend that I never asked for, the one that I didn't know I needed, and the one that eventually walked away.

Ironically, this newly posted photo was taken in almost the same location as the very first photo Cory took of me years ago, before we ever met. And so, it seems that in this last photo, we've come full circle to being strangers again. *Thank you for that, Universe.*

I don't know what to think. Rather than flattery (after all, it is a good photo of me, which is rare), I feel bamboozled. I didn't know that "bamboozled" existed in my vocabulary until just now. I don't know how else to describe this whirlwind of emotions, and that word found its way to the tip of my tongue. Bamboozled. *What has Cory done to me?*

I bury my head underneath my covers and count from ten, as if there's an answer waiting for me at the end of the countdown.

As it turns out, there isn't an answer waiting for me. Only more questions. I take my head out from under the covers and I look at my laptop screen again. And there it is. There's a caption that I didn't initially see. Right underneath the photo posted by Cory are these words:

I chose you first, and I will choose to choose you again and again.

Is there a word for beyond bamboozled? Sit tight, dear readers, as I search the Internet for a word that best describes the state that I'm in.

I'm back.

The word is: befuddlement. I am in a state of uncontrolled befuddlement, and I don't like it. My confusion is quickly followed by anger. I need answers and there is only one obvious person who can provide them.

CHAPTER 51

The photo that Cory posted of me was liked by many strangers online. Again, I am not flattered. Online flattery does nothing for me in the real world. I press the thumbs-down button so hard that my keyboard hits me back. Newton's Third Law never fails.

I call Cory. He, surprisingly, picks up.

"Tell me where you are," I demand. He will feel my wrath today. *What a confusing mother-f—*

"I'm outside," he says.

My anger is bulldozed by this surprise.

I open the door and he walks in as if he lives here.

"How's it going?" he asks. His calm and casual demeanor makes my anger rise again. He sees I'm unamused; his smile quickly fades as soon as our eyes meet.

It wasn't too long ago that I was leaving a trail of tears all over this apartment because of him (and by "long ago," I mean up until last night). And now, here he is standing in my living room revisiting the crime scene like some sick psycho. (That was redundant—all psychos are inherently sick).

We stand in the middle of my tiny living room, which is just two feet from my front door. My tight living quarters force us to breathe each other's air, which is heavy with tension. Forced closeness is not what I want right now. Thank you to this city and its high cost of living.

Back to Cory.

I stand there and shrug my shoulders at him. I don't know what to do with all of this—his unexpected visit, his abrupt departure from work, *that* photo. It's too much too fast and I have no words.

He mouths to me "I'm sorry," as if it's a sentiment that is too heavy to vocalize.

My heart implodes.

"Why did you leave me?" I ask out loud and suddenly. I meant the question in the most general sense, not just in regard to his withdrawal from work. He withdrew from *me* and the space *around* me. He left me on an island that got aggressively lonely, while feeding me a crumb every once in a while. That is the best metaphor I can come up with considering my state of…whatever this is—uncontrolled befuddlement (*thank you, Internet Dictionary*).

Cory puts his hands on both of my shoulders and guides me to sit on the couch. He then takes a seat in the armchair next to me. Our knees are practically touching.

That smile of his is yet to return, and there is no reason to expect that it should considering the way his eyes keep falling to the floor.

I am aching for him to say something—anything—yet he doesn't. Again, I feel the anger rising. I don't want to do this anymore. He is wasting my precious vacation time.

I abruptly get up. "I'm going back to bed."

His hand suddenly grabs hold of mine. He pulls himself onto his feet and meets my eyes.

"You have every right to be upset," he says as his hand remains clutched around mine. "I wanted to run to you so many times, but I couldn't. When I'm with you, I'm happy—*too* happy. It's terribly confusing to feel happiness when I have this feeling of never-ending sadness looming over me. It's conflicting and complicated."

He looks at me pleadingly. He's searching for some understanding, some empathy.

I feel crushed. He's going through a lot with his mom's ongoing battle with cancer and here I am selfishly thinking about myself and my need for attention. I'm immediately ashamed that I let my emotions get to this point. I'm not the center of his world; I'm humbled by this reminder that big feelings can be so insignificant in the grander scheme of things.

His sad eyes are glistening as the mid-morning sun shines through my window. The spotlight finds its way onto him as it usually does. Cory brings the light wherever he goes.

"You…" he says slowly, "are a feeling that I crave. You are a feeling that I want to bottle and protect. I cannot keep away from you any longer. Please let me stay by your side."

This. This right here, is a moment that I wish to bottle and protect.

I put my hand to his face. He rests his cheek against my palm. I have no words. I missed my friend and I want to savor this moment now that he is within reach again.

My body finally registers that I'm tired. I feel the somber atmosphere suddenly weigh down on my shoulders and I'm ready to cave in to the feeling of exhaustion.

"I'm going back to bed," I tell him.

He doesn't say anything. That's expected. What can anybody say after that?

I walk off towards my bedroom, which is only a hop away from where we stand. Then I hear from behind me, "Can I come with you?"

Those words stopped my entire being from existing.

CHAPTER 52

We are coming to the end of my story, dear readers. Well, not exactly the end *the end*, but we are near the end of this chapter in my life.

Cory's mom passed. There is no easy way to break that news, so I'll just insert it here. She passed shortly after Cory quit the family's company, the one his mom built when it was just a one-woman show.

Young, eager, and outrageously smart, Angela Lee was determined to be her own boss. I wish I could have just an iota of her fire. I, on the other hand, can barely light my own stove on the first try.

My mind is all over the place as I stare out of my office window. Ever since Cory quit, this place has lost its light. Don't get me wrong—it's not all doom and gloom here. I have a great boss (Stan) and the work keeps me challenged. I'm content here. But do I want to spend all my hours at work? The answer is an unequivocal no. Multiple exclamation marks included.

I never questioned Cory about why he quit (in fact, I still don't know what exactly he did here in the first place). I trust him enough, however, to know he did what he thought was best for him.

It wasn't until later that he admitted—casually and in passing—that I had a heavy hand in his reason to quit. He didn't want my professional efforts to be minimized or tainted by the image of "us" at work. Favoritism at work is real and even the appearance of it could be damaging to one's professional career.

I understand the logic behind Cory's departure, but I'm still uncertain whether it was honorable or simply stupid. He must think I really care about this job. I suppose I do, but I cared more when he was here.

I should be flattered. After all, no one has ever quit a job for me. I couldn't even get my exes to take an extended vacation from work when we were together. Let me remind you, I have a track record of dating very hardworking men, one of which I almost married, and that didn't work out, did it?

I stare at the window in the office building directly across the street. The reflection at this time of day makes it hard to see who or what is behind that window. As usual, I wonder who might be on the other side of that glass. I wonder if they see me when I'm eating lunch at my desk, when I'm playing Solitaire, or when I'm pacing around mindlessly within these four walls as I wait for the end of the workday to come. Or, maybe no one really pays attention to the stranger in the building across the street.

That seems more likely.

My eyes refocus and I catch a reflection on the inside of my own windowpane. I jump. I turn around and it's Stan who has just entered my office.

"I told you countless times, Stanley Edwards, you need to make noise when you enter!" I exclaim. "You know that I get scared easily!"

He doesn't apologize. I guess after apologizing so many times—and forgetting my simple request to make some noise—he no longer feels the need to offer apologies. Instead, he smiles with amusement to himself.

"Do you want to go to lunch today?" he asks. "New place just opened up downtown."

Stan. He's the last thing that is keeping me tied to this job (besides the money). I say this again and again: employees don't quit their job, they quit their boss. I don't see myself quitting Stan.

I glance at the wall clock. "Actually, there's somewhere I need to be."

* * *

I wait outside of the airport terminal for arrivals. Countless passengers walk by. I love people-watching at this location. Some people walk outside to the curb for a cab; some people stop to read the gate information for their connecting flight; my favorite, however, are the ones that walk directly into the arms of someone waiting for them to come home (if they are lucky enough to have someone waiting).

Cory sprints as soon as he spots me in the crowd of people. He makes his way directly into my arms (lucky him). This is the first time I've seen him in months. The last time was at his mom's funeral.

When Angela Lee passed, Cory had lost everything—the only woman in his life for twenty-eight years. In fact, she was the only *person* in his life; it was at his mom's funeral that he met his dad for the first time—ever. That last sentence is heartbreaking, isn't it? It saddens me to relive that scene in my head.

As much as I wanted to hold onto him at that time, I knew he had to find peace after her passing. Only he could give himself that. And so, I gave him the space to find it—in whatever form his peace may manifest.

His journey took him to places he never been, to meeting people who he wouldn't normally meet, and to feeling things on levels he never felt. I waited until he was ready to come back to the familiar. I waited, not knowing if his journey would ever take him back to us.

And now, he's here.

"I'm home," he whispers as he wraps his arms around me.

My eyes start to well as I finally feel the warmth of his embrace. I pour myself into him. May the feeling of this moment be relived, revived, and never taken for granted. I'm in the arms of my person again. The emotions are overwhelming, and they compound with every passing second as if to convince my brain that this moment is real.

It is. He *is* really here. I feel him; I smell him. It's sensory overload. The tears are now fully formed and running down my cheeks as if they have places to be.

Cory holds my face between both hands as he examines me closely. "Are those happy tears or is something wrong?"

I'm bawling now.

The concern on his face is painfully clear and persistent. He tries to read my eyes for an answer. I gather myself and then finally whisper the words that he did not expect to hear—words that I've held in for months.

CHAPTER 53

"You are going to be a dad." I've been waiting to utter those words to Cory since I found out that I was carrying his child. But with his mom passing shortly after, I had to give him the time and the space to grieve before disrupting his life forever. People need to grieve properly; we can't rely on a stimulus—like the surprise of becoming a parent for the first time—to fill the void. It's a temporary pause, not a solution, to healing.

I look at Cory and I see all the good things that this world has to offer. He's the only one to ever call my bluff (I'm not as cynical as my inside voices are). Surprisingly, I failed at repelling him with my glass-half-empty attitude and my lack of enthusiasm for…most things in life, especially if they involve crowds.

Truthfully, he makes me want to be a better version of myself. I recognize the micro-changes that have happened in my life since he's entered it. Goodness follows him. Goodness *is* him. I have hope for the future.

He's going to be an amazing parent, just like his mother was.

We are still standing right outside of the arrival gates. Barely reacquainted and I drop this bomb on him. His eyes are red from trying to hold back the tears. He holds my hands in his. I feel the warmth in them as he grips mine tighter.

"Thank you for choosing me," he says barely audible. He pulls me in closer. How that is even possible is a mystery; the space between us is nonexistent. I'm on my toes as I try to lift my head above his shoulders to avoid suffocation. "You love me, don't you?" he asks.

I shrug with the little room I have for any kind of movement. "What is love, anyway?"

I can hear him sniffling. The tears have made their way out of his eyes and down his cheeks and nose. I pull away and take a good look at him. "Did I hurt your feelings, you fragile little butterfly?"

He chuckles. "All the time." He quickly reels me back into a suffocating hug. I am barely breathing in this embrace, but I would not want it any other way.

And then one somber moment later, he adds, "I just wish my mom knew about her grandbaby."

* * *

I walk back into work after I dropped off Cory. These halls have taken on new life. The walls seem more vibrant than they did just earlier today. The air is different. My stride is different. I dare say there is some serious pep—some purpose—in my walk towards my office.

I walk past Stan's office first. I wonder if he's eaten. I poke my head into the doorway.

"I can hear you singing before you even entered the building," he says to my floating head. An astute observation for someone who has tunnel vision during work hours.

"Have you eaten?" I ask.

"That new place was good. We should go there next time."

"We will." I leave him as he was.

I stroll into my office, almost doing a perfect pirouette before sinking into my desk chair. It seems inherently wrong to be this happy at work, a place that normally devours joy. And yet, it's possible. Being happy at work—what a concept!

I turn my computer back on. However, instead of diving right into work, I spin around (and around) in my chair. I then use my feet to push myself off the walls while still seated in my chair. I roll back and forth between the walls, one of which is adjacent to Stan's office. I'm sure he hears the sound of my wheels scraping the floor.

He knocks on our adjacent wall. "Get back to work!" he yells from his office. Yes, he indeed heard me rolling around in here.

Instead of doing what my boss just told me to do, I roll myself out of my office and I shuffle my way next door. Stan is already staring at me as I make it into the doorway of his office— still seated. His face tells me that he was expecting my interruption, as he should after barking such orders at his most productive employee. The audacity!

Regardless of the interruption, he greets me with a smile. He looks amused by my grand entrance.

"I want to remind you, Boss, that I know it looks like I'm slacking off over here"—I roll myself closer to his desk—"but I've already submitted two proposals earlier than the given deadline…and it's only Wednesday."

He does not immediately say anything.

And so, I roll myself back and forth, gaining momentum by pushing my feet off the walls, just like I did in my own office moments earlier.

He tries to stifle his smile with tightened lips. He folds his arms across his chest and looks down. I made a good point, he must admit. When he looks up again, he simply says, "You look happy."

"I am. It's a weird look, right?"

Suddenly, something outside catches my eye. I stop my chair-rolling Olympic game. I immediately walk up to the large window behind Stan's desk.

There's a sign in the window of the building directly across the street from us. Stan gets up and sees it too. The handwritten sign reads:

Today must have been a good day!

I wonder if it was my whimsical twirling or my carefree chair-rolling that gave it away. I wonder how long these anonymous people-watchers have studied us and what kind of stories they've made up about us from afar.

So, it turns out, they *can* see us from across the street (*good to know*). I hope they had a few good laughs watching this shitshow.

Stan and I smile at each other. An unspoken understanding passes between us; this shitshow isn't so bad. The good days will come.

We go back to standing as we were, looking out of this glass window at a sign made by complete strangers. It's ethereal that people whom I've never met could bring a smile to my face from a distance away.

Today was a good day indeed.

Just like today, my story and your stories are made up of moments—moments that occur in between the mundane, the routine, the ordinary. It's these in-between moments, wedged between bookends of the seemingly boring, when emotions become amplified, and consequently, *remembered*.

Here I am at work, a place that sucks the life out my plants (and me), and yet I am surprisingly happy. I recognize the effect of the company I choose to keep—or the company that chose me—like Mary, like Stan, like Cory, all of whom created moments in my life that are worth retelling (even in a soul-sucking place like this).

I gently place my hand over my belly. Now, she may not have chosen me, but I will choose to choose her forever. She was made in these in-between moments.

She will be the story I tell and retell.

EPILOGUE

I stand in the corner of the hospital room as I watch Cory watch his mom, who is laying on the bed hooked up to various machines and drips. I don't know the technical term for all of this equipment, but the sight of them hooked up to a frail body incites fear for the worst. It's a daunting scene to see the fierce Angela Lee at her weakest. The fluorescent hospital lights create dark shadows in the hollows of her cheeks. Her eyes, however, still beam as she looks at her only son.

I can see the physical strain on Cory's hunched body. It's an enormous weight to sit bedside with imminent loss. I'm here to support him, yet I cannot offer any comfort. A hand on the shoulder may break him. I don't take that risk and so I refrain from reaching out, but I hurt *for* him.

The room is quiet except for the sound of multiple monitors beeping.

"I'll go get us some coffee," I say in an attempt to excuse myself. This is an intimate moment that feels almost wrong of me to witness. They should have the space to live in this moment uninterrupted.

"No, I'll get it," Cory says hastily.

I understand why he volunteered. He rushes out of the room, but not fast enough for me to not see the tears streaming down his face. My favorite person is hurting, and I am rendered useless in this situation.

I don't know what I should do here. I remain standing with my back against the door. I look around the room unsure of the best place to rest my eyes. They finally land on Angela. She smiles at me. Her smile is faint, but resilient.

"Life," she simply says as she manages to give a slight shrug with her shoulders.

I remain silent and nod—reluctantly. When there is no other explanation for why bad things happen to good people, I give it up to "life" being the unkind, inconvenient, unfair son of a— well, you get the point.

She gestures for me to sit on the chair beside her bed. Before I even sit down, she grabs my hand and holds it between hers.

In this cold hospital room, it's a relief to feel her warmth.

"Please continue to be his friend for when I'm gone," she says barely above a whisper. "I hope he's never alone."

My heart drops somewhere onto the floor. The feeling is so great that it escapes me, and I'm left numb in my seat. I heard what she said, but I cannot accept what she said.

My throat is dry.

Once oxygen makes its way back into my brain, my body begins to *feel* again. The feeling of inescapable heartbreak takes over and wreaks havoc on my senses.

I lay my head down with my forehead touching the back of Angela's clasped hands.

Deep breaths. I need to tell her. Now.

I take a second to compose myself and then the words just fall out. "Cory will be a dad," I say as I nod my head vigorously as if to convince myself that this is real. It is, and she deserves to know. "He's going to be an incredible one, at that. He will never be alone. Ever."

Her eyes roam down to my stomach, and I can feel her gently squeezing my hand a few times. She closes her eyes as if my news is too much to handle. The tears form small puddles underneath her eyelashes, and then they begin to descend slowly down her cheeks when they are too heavy to hold their form.

She doesn't stop squeezing my hand.

* * *

One day later, Angela Lee passes.

AUTHOR BIO

Gina Pham was raised in the Bay Area. She currently resides in Benicia, California with her husband and three kids. As a child of first-generation immigrants, she followed the coveted college-then-corporate-career route. After stifling her desire to become a writer for years (and after finally losing her mind from endless hours of staring at spreadsheets), she decided it was time to write again—for her sanity. This debut novel was written under the duress of unemployment, but more importantly, fueled by her life-long dream of becoming a published author. If you purchased this book, the author thanks you for playing a role in shaping her dream.